John Lathern

The Hon. Judge Wilmot

A biographical sketch. Introductory sketch by D.D. Currie

John Lathern

The Hon. Judge Wilmot
A biographical sketch. Introductory sketch by D.D. Currie

ISBN/EAN: 9783337013325

Printed in Europe, USA, Canada, Australia, Japan

Cover: Foto ©Raphael Reischuk / pixelio.de

More available books at **www.hansebooks.com**

THE
HON. JUDGE WILMOT:

A Biographical Sketch.

BY

REV. J. LATHERN.

INTRODUCTORY SKETCH BY REV. D. D. CURRIE.

REVISED EDITION.

TORONTO:
METHODIST BOOK AND PUBLISHING HOUSE.
HALIFAX:
METHODIST BOOK-ROOM.
1881.

INTRODUCTORY SKETCH.

BY REV. D. D. CURRIE.

THE story of a life that has been given to worthy enterprises, to noble endeavours, and that has been marked by many and varied successes, to the mind and to the heart is ever fresh and instructive. Such a life was that of Lemuel Allan Wilmot, which began in January, 1809, and reached its earthly termination on the twentieth day of May, 1878. It has been deemed advisable, therefore, that a record of his busy and eventful life, and especially of his more prominent and important achievements, should be preserved. Though scarcely a paragraph from the pen of the departed Judge was available to assist the author in the preparation of these pages, yet other materials have been within his reach.* These he has carefully and successfully utilized in the volume before us.

From my earliest years, until the removal of Judge Wilmot from the scenes of earth, it was my privilege to look upon him under various circumstances and from different standpoints. When, in the town in which he lived, my boyhood years were gliding away, he was rapidly attaining prominence and popularity. He early acquired extensive fame as a barrister and as an eloquent pleader in the courts. He was then a central figure in the Legislature of New Brunswick. The memories of old electioneering campaigns, when the polls were open for sixteen days in succession, and at a later period for eight days, linger yet. Often, during these times, the wild fires of intense excitement burned fiercely enough. Though, on several occasions, violently and maliciously opposed, he was never defeated in an election. In the militia trainings, which in the present day are almost unknown, he was a prominent actor. And in most of the moral and social enterprises of the town he was an enthusiastic leader.

During the earlier part of Judge Wilmot's political

---

* Probably no other person has had facilities equal to those of Mr. Lathern for forming an accurate estimate of Judge Wilmot's inner-life and of his earnest purposes. For more than a score of years a very close intimacy existed between them.

career these Provinces passed through an important crisis. For a half century the Province of New Brunswick had been under the sway of an intolerant and irresponsible family-compact Government. The statute-book was stained with enactments involving invidious distinctions, adverse to the rights and liberties of so-called " dissenters," and " dissenting " ministers. During the first fifty years of the history of New Brunswick no "dissenter" was honoured with a commission as a Justice of the Peace—except under very ordinary circumstances. In the earlier part of his political career a change was working in the public mind in these Provinces. He was the mouth-piece of his time in New Brunswick. His period furnished him with materials. There were social and political forces at work, and he was borne on by them. Behind him was a mighty impulse; he was the man of the hour; and he was true to the call of right, and of duty, and of God. Bravely he battled for larger liberty and for "responsible government." Fiercely he was assailed by foul slanders of various kinds. But the principles for which he contended were triumphant; and, for himself, he won a permanent place on the roll of his country's greatest men.

Judge Wilmot possessed almost all the qualities which are indispensable to oratory of the highest merit.

His greatest defect, perhaps, was that he did not use
his pen enough. He had a commanding presence. He
had a rich, ringing, orotund voice, possessing great
volume and strength. His memory enabled him to
recall facts and incidents with great facility. His
imagination was equal to any emergency. He was
earnest, impulsive, enthusiastic. He was a master of
fiery and brilliant invective; and, when an extraordinary occasion demanded, could with tremendous vigour
wield against an assailant the fiercest weapons of sarcasm or ridicule. He did not confine his reading and
his studies to one profession or to one department of
life. He rather preferred a wider range of investigation and research. He had broad views of great
questions. While, sometimes, there was an impulsive-
ness and rashness in him, still mature deliberation led
to his recognition and acknowledgement of the truth
on all sides. He would listen to novel propositions,
weigh them candidly, dispassionately, and purely upon
their merits. He would never contend for dogmas
because they were old, nor for political parties because
they were respectable. For the *truth* he sought. The
truth he never would abandon. And, probably, if
need had been at any time, he would for the truth
have laid down his life.

As a barrister he was accustomed to rest his arguments on a few leading general principles of right, and truth, and justice, giving but little attention to what he regarded as the smaller points of his case. In political life he disliked manœuvres, side issues and flank movements; and preferred direct assaults, and an open battle, on a fair field. Although these qualities were sometimes not the most successful, and involved delay if not defeat, yet in the end with thinking men they gave him popularity and power. And they brought victory to the cause for which he contended.

To have been associated with Judge Wilmot as a member of his Society class, as a teacher of his Sabbath-school, and in later life as a pastor for three years of the Church in Fredericton, in which he held several important positions, is regarded by me as one of the highest privileges both of my early and mature days. During those three years he was the Lieut.-Governor of the Province. He was one of the most considerate, kindly, and sympathising church members with whom at any time it has been my privilege to be associated. No man could more easily recognize defects in pulpit efforts; none could more quickly perceive the chief purpose of a preacher's heart; and none would more generously make proper allowances for the difficulties with which an earnest teacher had to grapple than he. As the Superintendent of the Sabbath-school, as a class-leader, as the leader of the choir, and in other positions as a church-member, his fidelity, his consistency, and his gentleness, were a perpetual example and an inspiration.

According to inspired Isaiah, the Lord, sometimes in judgment, gives to a wayward or a rebellious people weak men for rulers ; and, at other times, in his loving kindness, he gives " the mighty man, and the man of war, the judge, and the prophet, and the prudent, and the honourable man, and the counsellor, and the eloquent orator." Judge Wilmot was an agent raised up by the Supreme Ruler to perform an important work. The genius, the fair-mindedness, the fervour, the pathos, the Christian simplicity, and the splendour of his long and useful life, in the State and in the Church, are not memories merely, but influences,—permanent lights and forces which have helped to mould the life of many who have passed away, and which are still shaping the destinies of many now living. This book will, it is hoped, help to 'perpetuate not only the memory, but also the influence of that pure and noble life.

CONTENTS.

"Only I think it well, in lives from which we wish to learn, to look out for the *strong* points ; being confident that weak ones will reveal themselves."—*Rev. F. D. Maurice's Lecture on Edmund Burke, quoted from memory.*

BIOGRAPHICAL SKETCH

OF THE

HON. JUDGE WILMOT.

I.

PERSONAL.

" To such a name
Preserve a broad approach of fame."
—Tennyson.

THREE thousand years ago the tower of David was built for an armoury wherein were hung, in thousands, the shields of his mighty men. Like the battle-flags in Westminster Abbey, consecrated by proud historical recollections and associations, they were preserved as memorials of inspiring heroic deeds. Athenians and Spartans, after the battles of Marathon and Thermopylæ, felt that they had a nobler character to sustain and a grander destiny to work out. Ancient Romans were accustomed, in their halls and homes, in statuary, to preserve the forms and features of illus-

A

trious ancestors; and to them the sculptured marble was
an eloquent incentive to patient endurance and resolute achievement. Mysterious and moulding influences,
and the potent energy of example and sentiment, were
not limited to sacred and classic lands and races.
They are common to every age, and run along the
whole line of our being.

"It is a homage due to departed worth, whenever
it rises to such a height as to render its possessor an
object of attention, to endeavour to rescue it from
oblivion; so that when it is removed from the observation of men, it may still live in their memory, and
transmit through the shades of the sepulchre, however
faint, some reflection of its living lustre."*

Amongst the most distinguished of our colonists,
by common consent, was the Honourable Judge Wilmot
—the subject of this sketch. "He possesses," according to contemporary and competent estimate, "brilliant
powers; and as a public speaker ranks with the most
eloquent in British America." †

There have been two groups of men—the Puritan
settlers of New England and the United Empire Loyalists—in whom we recognize the stamp of the very
highest qualities of mind and manhood, and of unself-
ish heroism; and the best blood of both these classes
was in his veins. By one line of lineage he was of
direct descent from the men who first touched Ply-
mouth Rock: "I traced my ancestry," he said, "to
those who landed on the shores of New England in

* Robert Hall.   † N. A. Review.

the *Mayflower*." He was also a descendant of the United Empire Loyalists—those heroic men and women, exiles of the Revolution, who, feeling that they could not sever themselves from the traditions and flag of their own proud nationality, from the unbroken forests of Nova Scotia, New Brunswick, and Ontario, undauntedly hewed homes for themselves and their children; and again, as with the Pilgrim Fathers,

"The sounding aisles of the dim woods rang
To the anthem of the free."

"Our United Empire Loyalists kept their loyalty during seven long years of conflict and suffering; and that loyalty, with courage and enterprise, and under toils and privations unsurpassed in human history, sought a refuge and a home in the wilderness of Canada, felled the forests of our country, and laid the foundations of its freedom and prosperity."*

The vital principle of attachment to the laws and institutions of the land in which we live, veneration for a constitution and government that guarantee the fullest measure and perpetuity of civil and religious freedom, the healthy glow of race and nationality, and of proud ancestral achievement, with deeply cherished traditions and convictions, became the most potent moulding force in many a loyalist's colonial home.

From the ardent patriotism by which L. A. W. was always distinguished, it might almost seem as if the

---

* Dr. E. Ryerson, vol. II., pp. 449.

spirit of all the Loyalist race had come to him as a rich ancestral dower.

Lemuel Allan Wilmot was born January 31st, 1809. His native place was Sunbury, on the St. John River, the first home of many Loyalist families in the Province of New Brunswick. He was a son of William Wilmot, Esq., member of the Legislative Assembly, and grandson of Major Lemuel Wilmot,* formerly of the Loyal American Regiment, who settled in the Forest Province.

Colonel Murray, known to the older residents of St. John, grandfather of Hon. R. L. Hazen, of whom a fine oil painting, by Copley, is preserved in the Hazen branch of the family, was the great-grandfather of Hon. L. A. Wilmot. The gallant colonel was on the Royalist side in the revolutionary war, which by all Loyalists was regarded as rebellion. He had, on one occasion, a narrow escape from capture by Colonial troops. Foiled in their search, a bayonet was run through his portrait—the gash of which can still be seen.

* The first instalment of Loyalists reached St. John—then Parr's Town, chiefly covered with scraggy spruce and swamp—May, 1783. About five thousand, and amongst them Major Lemuel Wilmot, landed that summer at the same place. They mostly settled along the banks of the St. John River, as far up as the mouth of the Nashwaak. The opposite point, where Fredericton now stands, and which was scarcely reached by the first wave of immigration, was known as St. Ann's. There still stood the forest primeval. The whole country was known as Sunbury, county of Nova Scotia. In November, 1784, the Province of New Brunswick was proclaimed, and the first Government organized, by Colonel Thomas Carleton, brother of Sir Guy.

The mother of Mr. Wilmot, sister of the late Judge Bliss, died when he was only eighteen months old. She was a lady of very superior intelligence, cultured mind and taste, and of pure and noble worth of character. He often touchingly alluded to the fact that he had never known, in his own life, the tenderness and sweetness of a mother's love; but, in her early departure from earth, felt that there had come to him a rich legacy of affectionate and prayerful solicitude. There is good reason to believe that varied and brilliant qualities were in a measure hereditary. Through several of its gifted members the family with which *maternally* he was connected claimed considerable distinction. His father, of whom it has been said that from memory he could recite the whole of Dr. Watts' hymns, was a hymnodist before the days of hymnology; and in this fact may be found an explanation of the poetic taste of his more gifted son.

The earliest fact of L. A. Wilmot's boyhood which has come under notice was attendance at Government House, for the purpose of receiving instruction in music and singing, with a view to service in the choir of Christ Church. He was trained personally by Lieutenant-Governor Smythe. The early advantage thus afforded was doubtless an important contribution to the cultivation of gifts that were afterwards nobly consecrated to the service of the Church.

Before entering college, while habits of life were in their first formative process, Lemuel was sent to reside for a time in a purely French community.

The primitive simplicity, gentle and truthful manners of the *habitants* had for him a special charm; and, from natural temperament, he was peculiarly susceptible to influences with which he was now in close and constant contact. To the last there were vivacity of speech and animation of gesture that may in part have been due to the moulding force of life at Madawaska. During that time he heard and spoke only one language; and, if not for purity of style, for the excellence attained in its use, and for ease and flow of expression, he may have been indebted to that early educational advantage. It has been mentioned by a gentleman of distinguished professional eminence, who accompanied him on a visit to Laval University, that priest and professor were charmed with their visitor; and that, conversing in French, there was all the ease, fluency and vivacity of one "to the manner born."

The University College at Fredericton afforded valuable educational facilities. In his collegiate course he earned the reputation of a diligent and successful student. The Greek and Latin Epics, the Iliad of Homer and the Æneid of Virgil, which he is said to have read with exact and pure accent and quantity and smoothness of elocution, were a source of unmingled mental gratification. He also achieved the then scarcely less coveted and reputable distinction of being "the best swimmer, skater, runner, wrestler, boatman, drill-master, speaker and musician" of the time. From his *Alma Mater*, on which his eminent career reflected lustre, he subsequently received the honorary degree of D.C.L. In 1834, having but recently been admitted to the Bar, he was enthusiastically elected to the House of Assembly, and was for many years the leader of the Liberal party.* In 1844 he became a member of the Executive Council; and for three years, from 1848, was Attorney-General and Premier of the Province. He "attended, with Sir Edmund Head, a meeting of the Canadian Government at Toronto on colonial questions; and again, at Halifax, of the Governments of Canada, Nova Scotia, and New Brunswick, on the subject of collegiate reform. In 1849 he consolidated the criminal laws of the Province; and in 1850, the laws relating to towns, counties and parishes."† In 1851 he was appointed one of the Judges of the Supreme Court; and under the Act for the Federation of the Colonies into the Dominion of Canada, 1868, in recognition of valuable public services, and of commanding and conspicuous qualities of intellect and character, was made the first Lieutenant-Governor of his native Province. He was also, in association with Palmerston, Gladstone, and other eminent men, a Vice-

* Through courtesy of J. W. Lawrence, Esq., of St. John, as these pages are passing through the press, several dates have been communicated : L. A. Wilmot "was admitted attorney, 1830 ; barrister, 1832; elected 'for York County, on death of Wm. Taylor, June 16, 1834 ; delegate to England shortly after ; Attorney-General, on death of Hon. C. J. Peters, May 24, 1848 ; delegate to Portland R. R. Convention, 1850 ; candidate for last time, 1850 ; appointed Judge, on resignation of Chief Justice Chipman, and elevation of Judge Carter, January 8, 1851."

† *Vide* "Parliamentary Companion."

President of one of the leading British institutions;
successor of the Rt. Hon. Mr. Childers, M.P., on the
Prince Edward Island Land Commission; a member
of the University Senate, and gave much time and
thought to the promotion of educational interests.

Another department of public service, to which
great importance was attached, and in which brilliant
distinction was achieved, claims a fuller notice. He
was Lieutenant-Colonel of Militia, and always found
time for efficient drill. Considering the enthusiasm
carried into all military exercises, it would not have
been surprising had he adopted that profession. A
very natural remark of a Governor-General, on a visit
to Fredericton, received with military honours, was
that " he must have missed his calling, and should have
taken to the sword rather than the gown." With the
bearing of a superb cavalry officer, and a voice which
on parade ground rang out like the blast of a bugle,
he had all the qualities needed for command.

Militia training days, of which we hear nothing
now, were then greatly in vogue in Fredericton. They
were the gala days of the capital and surrounding
country. The old spirit of the Loyalist was then fully
awake. The national banner was proudly unfurled.
A band of music poured forth martial and popular
strains. The carriages of official and aristocratic families rolled grandly through the streets. For special
celebration an ox was roasted on the open square or
adjoining field, and it mended the cheer of the day. The
rank and file of militia carried their old-fashioned and

clumsy muskets. But the cavalry, in showy uniform and immense helmets, as they dashed from point to point, made a grand impression; and even their chargers, some of which had recently been released from dray or plough, showed to good advantage on that holiday parade. For the admiration of spectators, the rifles in green were rivals of the horsemen. But the artillery, stationed on the bank of the river, excited the keenest interest. Their operations looked like real war. The boom of cannon sounded as the roar of battle. The excitement culminated when, in mimic warfare, they had to defend their guns from a sudden onslaught of troopers. A sham fight on one occasion was arranged between the militia and regular soldiers of the garrison. In memory of a great battle fought over again on that day, the place of conflict, a little below the Cathedral, has ever since been named "Salamanca."*

In all militia movements L. A. Wilmot took a prominent part. He was, in later years, Colonel of the 1st York Battalion. He raised and commanded a troop of volunteer dragoons, that performed dispatch duty pending border difficulties, 1838-9. Communication was thus ensured between the capital and the frontier; and, at the same time, precautions were taken for the rapid blockade of any forest path through which a hostile force might seek to advance. He also organized and commanded a troop of dragoons for escort duty to the Prince of Wales on his visit to this

---

* "Reminiscences of an Old Inhabitant," in *Reporter*, Dec. 1st, 1880.

A*

country in 1860. The service was rendered in a style that challenged general admiration; and the Lieutenant-Colonel received, in the most cordial and gratifying form, the thanks of His Royal Highness. A cavalry corps trained by him was for a long time the pride of the city, and two men of that corps became afterwards colonels of cavalry in the army of the United States.

" The ex-Governor may be said to have been a public man all his life, for he had scarcely left the student's desk in the law office of Mr. Putnam, before the County of York elected him to a seat in the House of Assembly, and he at once gave evidence of that brilliancy of talent which made him conspicuous throughout the course of a very eventful career. He will ever be regarded as a most prominent figure in the political history of his country, and posterity never can thank him enough for the part he took in securing civil rights and liberties. These days were days of struggle that the present generation knows little about, and the Judge was always in the front of the fight. The seclusion of the Bench did not remove him from the eyes of the public, as he continued prominent as a lecturer and orator, and some of the best and finest efforts of his life were made during the years he wore the judicial ermine. Take him all in all, our country, perhaps, has never produced his counterpart. Of wonderful versatility, eloquent and mighty in speech, scathing and withering in sarcasm, sparkling, humorous and magnetic in conversation, the lamented ex-Governor seemed to stand one by himself. Before and since his death Royal honours have been heaped upon Canadians not half as much entitled to them for what they did for their country as he, and no provincialist ever more deserved a public monument at the hands of his countrymen. The illustrious part he took in the advocacy and accomplishment of Responsible Government alone entitles him to such a monumental recognition. If Judge Wilmot had been an American citizen, such a monument would long since have been erected to his memory, side by side with Daniel Webster and Henry Clay, either in Central Park, New York, or on Boston Common."*

It rarely falls to the lot of any distinguished colonist to act the varied part, or to discharge the multifarious duties, which devolved upon Hon. L. A. Wilmot. Yet, such was the splendour and versatility of gifts and of genius, that in each appearance upon the stage of public action, and through successive scenes, the impression produced upon spectators was generally that of signal and special qualification. But the highest fame achieved, in which he can scarcely be said to have had any successor, is mainly due to an extraordinary gift and power of *eloquence*. He had the advantage of a commanding personal presence—unfailing resource of speech, adequate to the widest range of political discussion—the instincts and intuitions of genuine statesmanship—readiness in debate and apti-

* *Fredericton Reporter.*

tude of reply—ability at will to wield a polished
weapon of satire—a brilliant wit, which, like the harm-
less summer lightning, for mere amusement, played
around the subject, or, in moments of intensity, gleamed
forth with sudden and scathing stroke—a magnificent
voice, in lightest whisper audible to any assembly, and
in impassioned declamation rolling into thunder-peal.
These were amongst the important qualifications which,
in any arena of statesmen and parliamentary orators,
ordinarily command proud distinction and ensure acknowledged success. By gentlemen who listened to his
great speeches in the Provincial Assembly—in contention for constitutional liberty and the overthrow of
monopoly—familiar with debates in the English House
of Commons, it has been asserted that never, according to their judgment, had his greater efforts been surpassed.

Where upon the bright roll of fame shall the
name of L. A. Wilmot find permanent record? Can
we challenge for him high and honourable rank
amongst the great and most gifted men of his country
and time? The reply may be found in answer to
other questions germane to the subject. By what
acknowledged standard must the value of life and life-
work be determined? What is the correct criterion
of greatness or of genius? Is it mental power? moral
worth? commanding influence? In what fineness or
purity of mold must the cast of such mind have been
taken? Is it essential to our ideal of greatness that
elements of inventive and constructive genius should
combine in given measure and equal proportion?

Ought affinities of mind and character to be of a nature sufficiently powerful to control and crystallize the active and moving forces and influences with which they may be brought into contact ? Is it an indispensable condition, that thrown to the front, when mediocrity sinks back to obscurity, he shall prove equal to the occasion ? Should not the mission of such a life be signalized in deepening the channels of human thought and broadening the boundaries of freedom ? Must not a prominent actor in a social and political revolution put the permanent stamp and impress of his mind upon the place and period in which he lives ? There have been few public men who, on the whole, had less reason to fear the application of searching, stringent test than had the leader of political reform in the Province of New Brunswick. In the old days of brilliant political debate, while the glamour of eloquence was still over the vision of admirers, few would have doubted the validity of his claim to an enduring distinction. The great work of his public life, however, and that by which its special value and permanent status must be tested and determined, has yet to be indicated. Were chiselled column or niche in trophied temple needed for national commemoration, it might be appropriately inscribed: *Executive Responsibility.* That great harmonizing principle of constitutional government, impressed upon the institutions of his country, carries with it an imperishable record:

> " A life in civic action warm ;
> A soul on highest mission sent ;
> A potent voice in Parliament ;
> A pillar steadfast in the storm."

In the course of this sketch, brief passages have
been culled from available published reports. These
specimens of eloquence have been reproduced, on this
memorial page, under considerable sense of restraint.
One cannot but feel, from the force of concurrent
testimony, that they convey but a poor idea of the
living orator, of the thunder that shook the Legislative
Hall, and of powerful appeals that roused listening
crowds to sympathetic action. Reports of political
speeches, as they appeared in Provincial papers of that
time, at the very best were meagre and unsatisfactory.
In the case of L. A. Wilmot, copiousness of style and
fluency of utterance constituted a special difficulty.
Expansion and amplification are essential to the success of popular or parliamentary oratory. When these
were mentioned as defects in the style of Pitt, the
great Commoner claimed that "every person who
addressed a public assembly, and was anxious to make
an impression on particular points, must either be
copious on some points, or repeat them, and copiousness is to be preferred to repetition." Mr. Wilmot had
the advantage of an opulent vocabulary. His oratory
had qualities of expansion ; and in this fact, as well
as in that spell of speech which few reporters could
resist, may be found an explanation of printed meagre-
ness. Fragments of speeches, such as have been preserved, are quite likely to furnish as accurate an idea
of an unknown writer's composition as of the affluent
style and pure diction of the honourable member to
whom they are assigned.

My own acquaintance with the Honourable Judge Wilmot dates back to the closing part of the year 1855. By Dr. Beecham of London, who in a recent visit to the Eastern Provinces had made his acquaintance, he was spoken of in the most appreciative manner ; and, in accordance with that competent and exalted estimate, a very high anticipation had been cherished. After a first cold sleigh-drive from the city of St. John—every incident of which has been indelibly impressed upon the recollection of that period, then recently arrived from England—a cordial welcome was received at Evelyn Grove. The Judge was then in the golden prime of life. Tall and straight in form, of light elastic step and graceful attitude—a rapid, searching glance—keen, restless, flashing eye—exquisitely chiselled features—a lofty forehead, firmly compressed lips, indicative of resolute purpose—a commanding presence and beaming kindliness of manner, accompanied by a ceaseless flow of sparkling speech, made up a most impressive and fascinating *personnel*.

In the admirably executed likeness by which this volume is accompanied, his personal appearance as delineated will be readily recognized. But it will also be apparent to all who were long acquainted with the subject, that the portrait belongs to a period of which it is said that "the almond tree shall flourish." There are the beauty and the blossoming of ripe and venerable years. Advancing age and excessive severity of nerve-pain wrought a marked change during the last decade of life. In any public effort that might be

attempted, instead of former vigour and elasticity,
there was rapid exhaustion of strength ; and, as the
consequence, sometimes a good deal of subsequent
suffering. The voice, once round, full, sonorous, became lighter and thinner in its range and volume.
The eye, though not dim, scarcely sparkled with its old
light and fire.   There were some other signs, not to be
mistaken, of growing physical feebleness. But still the
likeness is an accurate and a speaking one ; and, vastly
more than mere description, it is eloquent in expression.
Beautiful glow and benignity of countenance, well
brought out and retained in the work of the artist,
are a true and faithful index to commanding qualities
of mind and of character. As in the reflection of a
glowing lamp, through a delicate and transparent
vase, a pure light suffuses and softly rests upon the
finely-moulded features. But in earlier years, and in
the eager excitement of political or of professional
contest, there was a mobility of face that marvellously
corresponded with restless mental activity, and with
changeful moods of the moment. The brow, which
seems placid and serene as the summer morning, would
then at times gather to a cloud. In denunciation of
wrong, of injustice, or of falsehood, there was a well-
remembered expression that darkened into the severity
of strong indignation.

Retirement from the arena of politics at the
time of that visit referred to, release from professional
business pressure, and easy competence secured by his
elevation to the Bench, afforded opportunity for the

gratification of horticultural and literary tastes; and, such was the activity of mental constitution, exuberance of temperament and fluency of utterance, that all the passionate purposes and governing impulses of life were at once revealed. Never, has it sometimes seemed, was there such lavish expenditure of intellectual resource, and of wealth of conversation, as on those days of delightful and profitable intercourse. Then was mooted for the first time, as far as my acquaintance with the subject was concerned, the idea of a British American Federation to comprise all the Provinces from the Atlantic to the Pacific, and *Acadia* was the name suggested for the new nationality. There was also the more magnificent conception of an Imperial union. He believed, with Lord Durham, that "the British Colonies were like foreign nations to each other without any of the benefits of diplomatic association." But with Canada, Australia, India, and all the other Colonies united to each other, bound firmly to the Mother Country, constituting an Empire to comprise all British dominions, through which should course the same pulsation of constitutional life, over which should wave the same time-honoured national banner, there would be guarantee of security—for no part could with impunity be attacked; and there would be substantial economical advantages, for Imperial policy would be shaped with a view to the conservation and promotion of all varied interests. One of those projects, though at the time deemed a little visionary, has

already become an accomplished fact. What of the
possibilities of the Imperial idea?

From that time, in pastoral relation, while stationed in the city of Fredericton, in frequent visits, in
closely confidential friendship, in unbroken correspondence through all the years between, there has been
opportunity afforded for forming an estimate of his
life and character. That there were impulses, by
which at times he was borne along into imprudent
courses, was only too plain and a matter of regret to
his best friends; but these defects, almost inseparable
from the intensity and natural impetuosity of his
character, were all upon the surface. Those who knew
him best could most readily excuse an imprudence of
impulse, and could best appreciate the genuine worth
and the nobleness of soul by which he was always
distinguished.

In view of his representative character as a distinguished colonist; the rare and splendid gifts by which
he was so richly endowed, the wide space which for a
lifetime he filled in the eyes of the community; the
influential and responsible positions which long and
honourably he occupied; the forty years of continuous
service in discharge of political, judicial, and governmental duties; the high-toned principle uniformly
exhibited through the whole of his public career; the
consistency of his course and character through a
protracted and sometimes stormy life; the extent to
which many young men, now widely scattered, were
influenced by his generous impulses, intense enthusi-

asm, burning words, and deeds of noble, beautiful worth ; for the sake of still greater good, it has been much desired that there should be permanence and perpetuation of influence and of soul-stirring memories.

" One of the noblest characters in colonial annals is that of the late Judge Wilmot. As a statesman, a patriot, and a Christian, he was a man of shining mark. He had a cultured literary taste, and was a ready and forcible speaker, rising at times into a commanding eloquence of style. He was a man of tall and noble presence, of mobile intellectual features lit up with keen bright eyes. Amid the political conflicts of great constitutional crises, in which he was the foremost leader, he held high his name and fame, unaspersed even by the rancour of party strife. He was at once a great liberal leader, who guided his country into an era of constitutional liberty, and a man of staunchest loyalty to the person and crown of his sovereign. More than any man we ever met, he realized our ideal of the gallant Bayard, a *preux chevalier*—without fear and without reproach. He possessed in a remarkable degree the magic gift of successful leadership—the power of inspiring confidence, enthusiasm, and devotion in his followers and associates. No history of his native country can be complete which does not devote a large space to his work and influence. It is, therefore, especially beseeming that on his removal from the busy stage on which he has played so grand a part, the story of his life should be recorded, and its lessons gathered up as a permanent legacy for his Church and country. So many-sided was this life, through so many channels did it pour its influence, that it is only by looking at it from various aspects, and tracing these various channels, that one gets an adequate idea of its grand symmetry and multifarious activity."*

* Editor *Canadian Methodist Magazine.*

II.

PROFESSIONAL AND POLITICAL.

"That noble figure, every look of whose countenance is expressive, every motion of whose form is graceful, an eye that sparkles and pierces, and almost assures victory, while it speaks audience ere the tongue!"
—Brougham.

IN 1832, L. A. Wilmot—the initial letters of whose name formed the word LAW, and often in that style used for signature—having successfully and satisfactorily completed the requisite course of preliminary study, was admitted to the Bar of New Brunswick, and in 1838 was created Queen's Counsel.—It must not be supposed that, with all his brilliant gifts and splendid endowments, he could without difficulty conquer success. Though afterwards one of the most fluent of speakers, endowed with all the natural attributes of a consummate orator, and every grace of style and attitude, yet as a student, singularly enough, for a time he had to contend with impediment of speech. "What! you," his father is reported to have said, in reference to an early expression of preference for the legal profession, "with a stammering tongue, aspire to the dignity of a pleader!" But from the first there was the consciousness of power; and, if he could not be a Demosthenes, undaunted by an obstacle overcome by the most renowned of all orators, he aimed at the very highest distinctions of his chosen profession.

"There is no royal road to learning," he said, years afterwards, in one of his brief but brilliant Encenia addresses. "We speak not of the Empire, but of the *Republic of letters*. In this domain there are no hereditary honours. Distinctions can only be achieved by individual effort. Each competitor must win and wear." On that and similar occasions, in the same strain, he no doubt spoke from remembrance of early obstacles overcome by assiduous application. "With whatever faculties," says an eminent writer, "we are born, and to whatever studies our genius may direct us, *studies* they must still be. I am persuaded that Milton did not write his Paradise Lost, nor Homer his Iliad, nor Newton his Principia, without intense labour:

> Some will lead to courts, and some to camps ;
> To Senates some :

but, whatever the pathway of life may be, and whatever profession may have the preference, only by patient and laborious pursuit can the summit of excellence be attained."

The popularity which L. A. Wilmot achieved as a pleader was of a most unique and exciting character. In that lordly arena, where justice presides, the gifted and brilliant men who have coveted and contended for professional pre-eminence and distinction have not been few; but his influence with juries was more extraordinary, and his success in pleading more splendid, than that of any lawyer who up to that time had practised at the New Brunswick bar. The magnetism of noble and graceful personal presence; the fire, force and unrivalled felicity of forensic eloquence; the versatility and daring of genius; the faculty of cleaving a way straight to the core of the subject; a pathos which thrilled, melted and subdued; mastery of potent invective and power of terrific exposure, which, when concentrated into scornful and indignant denunciation of a mean and contemptible action, gleamed and scathed like forked lightning and rankled like a barbed arrow, were employed according to the exigencies of the case. They were all calculated to enforce legal argument, and to ensure a verdict in favour of his client. The fact has frequently been mentioned that during his practice at the bar he rarely lost a case. The very atmosphere of court, at other times serene and severely judicial, became charged with the electricity of his spirit and speeches; and, for the most grave and dignified Judge, it was not always easy to prevent or suppress demonstration of popular feeling, thrilled and moved by resistless eloquence, to sympathy or indignant scorn. "As an advocate at the Bar," says the writer of a brief sketch in a Boston paper, a valuable reminiscence, "few in any country could surpass him. The Court was full when it was known that Wilmot had a case. He scented a fraud or falsehood from afar. He heard its gentlest motions. He pursued it like an Indian hunter. If it bur-

rowed he dragged it forth, and held it up wriggling to
the gaze and scorn of the Court. When he drew his tall
form up before a jury, fixed his black, piercing eyes
upon them, moved those rapid hands and pointed that
pistol finger, and poured out his argument and made
his appeal with glowing, burning eloquence, few jurors
could resist him." There was nothing melodramatic
in his style or mental constitution; but not unfrequently
prompted by an impulse or intuition that the most
consummate áctor might have envied, but which without a measure of the same genius it would have
been dangerous to attempt an imitation, by a shrug of
the shoulder, facial expression, mimicry, or some tragic
tone, he would dexterously and successfully enforce
argument, cover retreat, or foil an opponent.

The secret of Mr. Wilmot's superb success at the
bar, and the influence which he wielded over almost
any class of men that could be empanelled, marvellous
as it seemed and almost magical to the crowds that
thronged the trial-scenes, is not far to seek. It was
mainly to be found in that quality of oratorical effort
which, born of the immediate occasion, somewhat excessive in embellishment and with not a few defects,
overmasters critical faculty, and achieves its purpose.
In dialectic skill and deep legal lore, during years of
practice, he doubtless encountered many a formidable
rival. But, in overwhelming force of appeal, and that
subtle sensibility of feeling which suffuses the speech,
evokes deep human sympathy, to which every mind
is strangely responsive, there was an indisputable su-

premacy. That oratory of the bar was ornate or emotional as the subject required. Sometimes professional exigencies called for severity of expression. The weapon which he. wielded was sharp as well as polished and glittering. He knew when to strip away mere rhetorical decoration and to use the naked edge. There was then plain and pointed Saxon phrase. A spade was a spade. Robert Hall's preference for *pierce*, to "penetrate," was commended as an ideal and law of terse and incisive speech. Legal subtleties were not permitted to perplex the minds of jurymen. Only salient points were brought into prominent view. If bored by bewildering *cases*, from the opposite side, there was forensic flash which shot athwart the dreary maze :

> "A countless myriad of precedent,
> That wilderness of single instances,"

known as English common law.

An incident of the Northern Circuit, without reference to any name, may be mentioned as illustrative of ingenuity and ready tact in professional emergency. The case was one of very considerable importance and involving large values. It was not in his judgment a promising one for his clients. In regard to the substantial merits of the matter in dispute he had no doubt. In a Court of Equity the righteousness of the claim could have been fairly established ; but on technical grounds, or because the *letter* of the law was adverse, he scarcely hoped for a verdict. There was a point upon which, as a pivot, the 'proceedings would

B

turn, and which would probably determine the result.
Complication warranted resort to stratagem. The
opposite counsel was a gentleman of great legal ability
and acumen, but occasionally hampered by an unfor-
tunate impediment of speech. The jury were assured
that his learned friend on the other side was eminently
upright and conscientious. Whenever this vital point
was reached—made so palpable to the jury that none
could mistake it—he would be sure to show signs of
embarrassment. The prediction was soon fulfilled. In
sight of the bird the fowler had set the snare. But
how to avoid it was the perplexity. There was manifest trepidity, and consequently defective articulation.
A titter of amusement could not be suppressed. Confusion became worse confounded; until, on that side,
there was a complete break-down, and Mr. Wilmot
gained the suit.

At that time, in the sister Province of Nova Scotia,
there were such lawyers as Stewart, Archibald and
Johnson. Their legal skill and eloquence were the
pride of their country, and would probably have commanded distinction at the British Bar. It was not an
unusual thing in New Brunswick, when any case of
great importance was pending, to obtain the advocacy
and assistance of one or more of those distinguished
barristers. Nothing succeeds like success. The simple
prestige of their names was almost sufficient to ensure
the result. When L. A. Wilmot began to make his way
up to professional eminence, and his influence felt at
the Bar, there awaited him the ordeal of rivalry with

these formidable competitors. It was only, however, in the keenest contest that the qualities that he possessed blazed out in all their splendour. That was a proud day for the profession in New Brunswick when, at fair tournament, he snatched the laurel wreath of success. And never at knightly tilt or the pride of feudal magnificence, where, amidst flash of gleaming steel and the glancing light of beauty, prizes were won and awarded, were there more eager spectators than on that occasion. When the forensic duel had been honourably fought, the case was committed to the jury. For a space, the Court adjourned. In the meantime, leading counsel on either side, on whom chiefly centred the excitement of the fray, returned to the hotel and retired for the night. But their slumbers were effectually disturbed by a loud legal hurrah. Junior members of the profession, cognizant of the decision, were disposed to make the most of their triumph. From that time the necessity for such importation has no longer existed. The mantle of the eloquent advocate has successively fallen upon many members of the same honourable profession in that Province.

Early in life Mr. Wilmot began to take part in the discussion of public questions. It has been told when, in response to an urgent call from the electors, he first took his stand upon the hustings, a gentleman of the ruling class rode up to the crowd. Counting upon sympathy as a matter of course, in deference to established order and as evidence of loyalty, the haughty official demanded that they should pull Wilmot down.

He would become Attorney-General of the Province !
The sneer was as a spark of gunpowder to a train
already prepared, and the signal for an unexpected
explosion. Lemuel Allan Wilmot, in person as commanding as in mental qualities, drawing himself up to his
full height, throwing the glove from his hand, began a
ventilation of public questions in a manner to which
the people had been little accustomed. The burst of
indignant eloquence, of denunciation, and of patriotic
appeal, was received by the crowd with thundering applause. " A champion of the rights of the people now
appeared, who was destined to lead his country into the
enjoyment of constitutional liberty."* From that day
he was looked upon as the tribune of the people and
the representative of popular rights. At an age when
most men aspiring to prominent position would still be
ranking as students, by " the irresistible voice " of
York electors, he was summoned into political life.
By acclamation, unprecedented in the annals of the
county, on July 31st, 1834, he was chosen member for
the House of Assembly. Parliament was soon after
dissolved. But at the general election which followed,
in December of that year, by the same influential con
stituency he was returned at the head of the poll.

They were stirring times in which L. A. Wilmot
made his entrance into public life. In Upper Canada,
where for a time collision between established conservatism and the spirit of progress had threatened
anarchy to the country, the cause of constitutional re-.

* *History of Canada:* Rev. W. H. Withrow.

form was steadily moving to victory. In Nova Scotia
the Legislature could boast a splendid galaxy of names,
not proportionately surpassed in the annals of any
Colony. The struggle for responsible government was
soon, in one of its phases, to commence in the famous
Howe libel case. Beneath the ægis of the British
Constitution there was *no padlock* for lips eloquent in
advocacy of progress and liberal principles. In Great
Britain a condition of almost chronic dissatisfaction
and of threatened revolution, under the able leadership
of Grey, Russell, Brougham, and others of scarcely less
celebrity, had been signalized by the inauguration of a
new and nobler era in liberal and progressive legislation. The Reform Bill belongs to that period. What
statesmen of the time were doing and daring in the
cause of national and political progress and freedom,
through other parts of the Empire, the patriotic member for York was emulous to attempt and achieve for
his native Province. "His political principles," he said,
in a later speech, "were not of yesterday. He had
gleaned them from the history of his country—a
country they were all proud to own. Would any
honourable member dare to tell him that because they
were three thousand miles away from the heart of the
British Empire, the blood of freemen should not flow
through the veins of sons of New Brunswick?"

The entrance of L. A. Wilmot into the parliamentary
arena, at that particular period, constituted an epoch
in the annals of the New Brunswick Legislature. "As
a debater he was for many years the chief attraction

of the House of Assembly. With imposing person, large forehead, handsome features, and keen eagle eye; with ready wit, cutting sarcasm, quick intuitions, enthusiastic declamation, a hearty sympathy with everything generous and good, and with scorn and hatred of every form of wrong, he wielded a potent influence."*

In parliamentary discussion he was a generous and honourable opponent. He only asked from others that which in return he was always prepared to give—a fair field and no favour. He was accustomed, by a single fearless bound, to plunge into the thickest of the fray. No consideration or claim of conventional custom ever prevented him from striking to the very heart of the question. The success of sheer artifice would not satisfy; and, in preference to flank movement, he generally faced the foe to the front of position. But he also wielded a keen-edged weapon of sarcasm; and, instead of elaborate speech, sometimes gained his point by a single dexterous stroke. Having occasion to expose groundless pretence, in merciless burlesque, and manner that was simply inimitable, there was Esop's fly that sat upon the axle-wheel of the chariot and said, "What a dust do I raise!"

The House of Assembly, in which for the first time Mr. Wilmot took his seat, met January 20th, 1835. The next day notice was given that he would call the attention of honourable members to the subject, then of international magnitude and importance, of the Boundary Line between the Province of New Bruns-

---

* *Zion's Herald*, Boston.

wick and the State of Maine. The time for *in extenso* reports of parliamentary speeches, and the enterprise of journalism now so conspicuous, had not yet come. But the measure of influence which, from the commencement, he wielded in that Assembly may be inferred from the boldness and vigour of tone in the discussion of constitutional questions—from extraordinary appointment on successive delegations to represent the House, of which he was the most youthful member, and which comprised a number of able and experienced politicians, in negotiation with the British Government on weighty matters of Provincial policy and of executive administration—from the fact, apparent from the official records of those years, that his name finds prominent place on nearly every important parliamentary committee.

Renewed attempts on the part of the Crown to establish a land-royalty, in the shape of *Quit Rents*, then a vexed and burning question through the country, the agitation of which had engendered great bitterness in the constituency of York, necessarily occupied much of the attention and time of the House of Assembly. The reservation had been regarded, in the first place, as simply an acknowledgment of sovereignty in the lands granted. The claim had long been suffered to remain dormant; and, in transfers of lands between individuals, the original reserve was no longer deemed an encumbrance. The determination to enforce payment would, it was believed, create widespread confusion, litigation, dissatisfaction, and distress. The fearless utterances of L. A. Wilmot, and his earnest and eloquent portrayal of the hardships which, without any corresponding advantage, enforcement of this claim would produce, especially upon the poorer settlers, and the "dismay." which would spread through the land, were ample fulfilment of previous pledges to his constitutents; and the County of York was warmly congratulated "on the choice of a representative so able and willing to protect the interests of the people."

During the parliamentary session of 1836, Mr. Wilmot moved an address to the Governor for a detailed account of the Crown Land fund. Sir Archibald Campbell, who had great aversion to the principles and progress of popular reform, and rather than submit ultimately resigned, sent down a mere general statement. The mover of the address was appointed on a mission to England.* The immediate object of the delegation, then an extraordinary event in colonial history, was to obtain for the representative Assembly the control of Crown Land rights and revenues—the main spoke in the wheel of compact administration—and to make the voice of the Reform party heard at the foot of the throne.

* With Mr. Wilmot, a very young politician, was associated an astute and experienced member of the House, soon after appointed to the Executive Council as Honourable Wm. Crane. In any game of artful policy he might be trusted to checkmate clever and wily opponents. But such was the contrast, that in after days the appointment was compared to the yoking up in the same team of a veteran charger, chafed with stiffness of age, and a fiery racer that spurned the bit and bounded for the course. On both delegations Mr. Crane rendered valuable service to the country.

The interest of a visit to the Old Country, for one of his romantic taste, cultured mind, and loyal pride of race and nationality—a young man twenty-seven years of age—cannot easily be described. By men of the Loyalist stamp that land was reverently and affectionately spoken of as *Home:*

> " The distant sea-girt isle
> Our fathers loved, and taught their sons to love,
> As the dear home of freemen brave and true."

It was the land of his ancestors and of a noble race whose blood flowed in his veins—the land of Shakespeare and Milton and Cowper, whose mother-tongue was his own, whose gems of beautiful thought and crystallized expression had enriched his ample and opulent diction—the land of Pitt and Burke and Erskine, whose burning thoughts and luminous eloquence, evoked and intensified by the supreme interest of the hour and occasion, he had studied until saturated with their spirit and sentiment—the land of proud achievement in arts and arms, and the home of that constitutional liberty for which, in a new colony, he and his coadjutors were resolutely contending*—the land of proud historic deed and of consecrated association—of stately and storied castle and pomp of cathedral architecture and magnificence. It was also

---

* " We must be free or die, who speak the tongue
That Shakespeare spake ; the faith and morals hold
Which Milton held."—*Wordsworth.*

B*

the seat and the scene of grand national pre-eminence,

> "The island home,
> Peerless among her peers ;"

and of that flag, the symbol of freedom under every
sky, which he had so often and so eloquently eulogized.

It was one of Judge Wilmot's maxims, in a letter
communicated in complaint and criticism of some
petty act of colonial administration, that "little
countries make little men." Unquestionably for him,
while still at the entrance of public life, for new and
nobler ideas and expansiveness of thought and sentiment, it was an immense advantage and an educational influence to breathe the air and mingle with
national life in its older and grander forms, and to
feel the stimulus of contact with the governing minds
of the nation.

From several distinguished members of the Melbourne
Cabinet the first New Brunswick delegation received
marked tokens of respect. There was one amiable
statesman, Lord Glenelg—better known as Sir Charles
Grant, whose portrait, chiefly because of the success
of that mission, and the introduction of a more liberal
governmental system, hangs behind the Speaker's
chair in the New Brunswick House of Assembly—who
took special interest in the youthful representative.

Lord Glenelg, at that time Colonial Minister, an
advocate of Liberal principles and a thoroughly upright
statesman, from extensive acquaintance with colonial
affairs and ample experience of official life, in relation

to the special object for which the delegation had been appointed, was competent to offer prudent counsel and in a position to afford valuable aid. In regard to personal and professional preference and promotion, where Crown patronage was concerned, he would willingly have pledged the fullest consideration. Had there been, on the part of the New Brunswick deputation, a disposition to negotiate for private advantage, that mission to Downing Street might have been turned to profitable account.

It was apparent also to members of the British Cabinet that the colonial politician possessed some rare qualifications—quickness of apprehension and a high order of eloquence—that might be turned to account in parliamentary debate, and which might contribute to the strength of the Liberal party in the House of Commons. A proposal was made that if he would remain in England a constituency should at once be found for him. It is useless now to speculate on what the achievements of his life might have been had he at that period, when habits of thought were still in formative process, consented to enter the Imperial Parliament.

It was a point with the delegation, remembering that the taunt of disloyalty had sometimes been the penalty of prominence in movement for popular right, to obtain presentation at Court; and, loyal to the core, the distinction was of a character to be thoroughly appreciated. Through the courtesy of Lord Glenelg, requisite permission was readily obtained and the details of Court costume speedily arranged. It may be safely asserted, that however brilliant and distinguished may have been the array on that occasion, there was not any one of more courtly presence and bearing than the untitled representative of an obscure Province. Ordinary regal etiquette was considerably disturbed when Mr. Wilmot was delayed and questioned by his Britannic Majesty concerning antecedents and family relationship. It was expected, of course, that with a brief answer he would gracefully retire. But, to the consternation of Lord Glenelg, unaccustomed to the freedom of impromptu speeches and trembling for the temerity of the attempt, impressed with royal condescension and determined to make the most of the opportunity, he burst the awful barriers of state; and, in loyal phrase, thanked His Majesty for generous consideration of Colonial interests. Probably the King (William IV.) was as much taken by surprise as the Colonial Minister. It was only, however, a passing incident; and, with but brief interruption, the order of presentation and procession was resumed.

There was not only delegation, but counter-delegation. Again, therefore, in 1837, with briefest notice, and a dreary winter drive by land from Fredericton to Bangor, the delegation was re-appointed to England. The result was all that, for the time, could be expected or desired. The Governor and Executive were compelled to yield the important matter in dispute. In consideration of a permament civil list, the control of valuable Crown land revenue was vested in the House of Assembly. The Lieutenant-Governor resigned; and Sir John Harvey, of conciliatory policy, the most popular of all the Governors sent out from home, was appointed as his successor.

At the Session of 1838, in consequence of the law-less invasion of Canada by an organized force from the American frontier, under pretence of sympathy with a company of colonial conspirators, an Act was passed by the New Brunswick House of Assembly, for which subsequently the special thanks of the Sovereign were received, authorizing the Lieutenant-Governor to call out and embody *twelve hundred* volunteers for service in British North America. In strenuous advocacy of this measure the patriotic spirit and enthusiastic loyalty of Mr. Wilmot found vehement expression. "This," he said, "was not a matter to be calculated upon mere pounds, shillings, and pence. It was to be viewed in connection with the relations which existed between this and the other Provinces. Their cause was ours !—the cause and battles of our brethren—of those very brethren who had fought side by side with them during the last war, who inhabited the same soil, who claimed connection with the same great and glorious empire, and who were now struggling against the efforts of wicked and seditious traitors and assailants. The Province, in aiding their fellow-subjects, would be fighting its own battles. Their cause was the same. The first shot fired in Upper Canada would reverberate to the utmost extent of the Lower

Provinces, and every loyal heart would thrill in response."*

Almost immediately following this expression of
enthusiasm, in 1839, consequent upon a threatened invasion of their own Province, the spirit of New
Brunswick loyalty was still more fully aroused, and
the chivalrous devotion of its people to the British
flag nobly exhibited. There was a disputed territory,
on the upper waters of the St. John river, that had
been invaded by lawless parties in search of lumber.
There had been resistance and armed collision. The
militia was sent from the State of Maine, and Governor
Fairfield made a call for ten thousand men. Two regiments from Fredericton were ordered to the scene of
strife. Sir John Harvey was resolved to defend the
right. New Brunswick volunteers flocked eagerly to the
national standard. The whole country was in a blaze
of excitement. That border warfare threatened for
a time to plunge the two nations into war. The Legislature of Nova Scotia voted £100,000 towards defence;
placed *twelve thousand* volunteers at the disposal of
the Commander-in-Chief; and then united in "three
times three cheers for the brave people of New Brunswick, and three times three cheers for the Queen of
England." "What had taken place in that sister
colony," said Mr. Wilmot, "would not only have a
grand moral effect in this Province; it would spread
throughout Great Britain; it would be heard and re-
iterated in the House of Commons; and they would

* *Courier*, January, 1838,

there perceive that in these colonies there were brave arms to defend the soil from the polluting foot of the invader, and hearts that could feel and appreciate the value of their connection with the Mother Country. It was well known that there was a party in the English House of Commons that would willingly barter away the inhabitants of these Provinces. The mouths of that party would be stopped. The people of England would not give up colonies where the inhabitánts, rather than pass under the dominion of a neighbouring nation, would die upon the soil where many of them drew their breath and where all lived happy and contented."

Duties of military drill, at that time, in preparation for threatened military struggle, alternated with scenes of political debate. "The stout hearts and nervous arms of New Brunswick deserved that discipline and direction without which they might encounter a foe to disadvantage." It was well known that L. A. Wilmot, qualified for command, intensely patriotic, in whose veins the old Loyalist blood ran as liquid fire, while urging the necessity for yeomanry drill, stood ready for active service on the frontier. Ultimately, however, for the weal of all parties, the matter in dispute was amicably adjusted and battle-flags were furled.* In a letter written by Hon. L. A. Wilmot, when Governor of New Brunswick, the old feeling had

---

* Arbitration, in which Lord Ashburton and Daniel Webster were the Commissioners, was substituted for cannon and the sword. The award of the Ashburton Treaty, made in 1842, yielded the most valu-

all subsided ; and he eulogises " the immortal words of President Grant : *Let us have peace.*"

It soon became apparent that, in an eminent degree, this youthful politician possessed the requisite qualities and equipment for successful leadership in another fight; and that upon parliamentary battle-ground, not in forest-struggle, would his most brilliant victories be achieved. Even before the contest for Responsible Government had commenced in thorough earnest, there was the presage of an approaching struggle. Like the muttering of distant thunder, ominous of gathering storm, arbitrary action provoked sharp and passionate protest: " When the Council takes such high and commanding ground," said the then recently elected member for York, "it is worthy of the representatives of the people to stand forth in bold relief; and, in the spirit of men determined to maintain their rights and liberties, to put their hands upon it at once, to arrest the career of wantonness of power, and to prove that we are indeed worthy of freedom and privilege and British rights." *

The system of government, at that time existing in New Brunswick and other Colonies, was that usually known as " the Family Compact." Offices of honour and emolument were monopolized by persons that had

able part of the disputed territory to the United States. There was a very general impression on this side of the line that the British nobleman was overmatched by the astute Republican statesman—that colonial claims were sacrificed to imperial interests.

* St. John *City Gazette.*

come out to the Provinces for that purpose. The Legislative and Executive Councils had in possession all governing power. They were almost exclusively and uniformly filled from classes claiming to constitute the aristocracy of the country. Members of the " Compact " were generally closely allied by family relationship or business association. Government was administered in virtue of what they regarded as an essential and inherent right of the ruling class. They only were supposed to possess requisite qualifications for official duty and legitimate claim to promotion. The patronage of the Crown, consequently, was dispensed and its power distributed within a narrow and favoured circle.

Crown officials were not in any way amenable to the representatives of the people ; and, in any case of remonstrance, members of that body were treated with but scant courtesy. For any gifted member of the Assembly to aspire to office, emolument, or governmental position, was deemed and stigmatized as evidence of restless, intriguing and even disloyal temper and spirit. Especially for any one who had evinced a disposition to disturb the comfortably established system, and who had the audacity to challenge the constitutional right and expedience of the dominant policy, there was not the slightest hope of preferment.

In combination with relentless conservatism, as the direct consequence of monopoly and intolerance, there was an attempt at ecclesiastical domination which by Dissenters, as then designated, was felt to be exceed-

ingly oppressive. For the offence of conducting occasional religious service on the Sabbath day, in a
spirit worthy of Star-Chamber and Stuart days and
dynasty, Mr. Wm. Wilmot, father of the judge, was
expelled from, or refused admittance to, his place in
the House of Assembly. There was no church established by law. Requisite statutory enactment had
not been secured. But as a fundamental principle
of Colonial Government, and one that was not likely
to be called in question, the theory of a State Church
was taken for granted. Equal rights of denominations were all but ignored. It was only about the
latter part of 1834, the time of L. A. Wilmot's election
to the House of Assembly, that the "Dissenter's
Marriage Bill" became the law of the land. The
object of that measure, wrenched from ecclesiastical
monopoly, mainly due to the diffusion of liberal ideas,
and the march of Reform then signalizing its triumphs
in Imperial and Colonial legislation, was to invest
dissenting ministers with legal authority to solemnize
the rite of matrimony. Even for members of their
own church or charge, up to that time, except under
the severe penalty of fine and imprisonment, these
clergymen could not officiate in any marriage service.
Against the deeply-shaded background of such facts,
by clear and correct perspective, we comprehend the
necessity for agitation—the advocacy of civil and
religious privilege. The opinion was afterwards expressed, during a discussion on "want of confidence"
resolutions, that had even the conservatism of 1836,

when the old official party sought entrenchment behind the prerogative of the Crown, been persistently adhered to, and carried out, "an insulted people would have risen in their majesty, and would have shaken off their yoke of bondage."*

The principles with which, from the commencement of his career, L. A. Wilmot was identified, and of which he was the most eloquent and authoritative exponent, were excessively obnoxious to the party in power ; and to the Government, as then organized, his speeches were regarded as a seriously disturbing element. As the champion of popular rights, he was sometimes in a vexatious manner charged with holding democratic principles ; and, notwithstanding the patriotic feeling which beat and throbbed through every sentiment and movement, in the bitterness and asperity of party debate was taunted with the taint of disloyalty. The imputation, however, could not turn him aside from the line of well-defined duty. He had the courage of his convictions ; and, in indignant and burning eloquence, meeting scorn with scorn, threw back the unwarranted imputation.

"Those who contended for liberal principles," he said, in one of those renowned field-days, then common enough in the New Brunswick Legislature, but which have no parallel in the tamer proceedings of modern parliamentary debate, " had their names covered with obloquy. They asked for a constitution that, while it protected the Queen upon the throne, threw, at the same

* Speech of Mr. L. A. Wilmot, 1847.

time, its paternal arms around the helpless infant. They asked for the pure, the free, the glorious constitution of England ; for this they had contended, for this the Liberals of New Brunswick had fought ; and let them call them *rebels* who had nothing else to write about, he cared not. They asked for a system that would give fair play to all, that would upset all Family Compacts, that would give the sons of New Brunswick their birthright—the benefit of free institutions and of self-government. He defied any honorable member to look at his political life and say where he had overstepped the bounds of the constitution. If he did live three thousand miles from the great body of the empire, still that empire sent its blood through the veins of every British subject. A son of New Brunswick had the same rights to the benefit of her institutions as a resident of London ; and he would not submit to be cut off by any political manœuvrings."*

The darkest hour—that which came just before the dawn of day, as ultimately proved—in that patriotic struggle seems to have been in the severely contested election of 1842. Then Mr. Wilmot, who for *eight* years had been a member of Parliament and the active and accomplished leader of the Liberal party, though now *only thirty-three years of age*, stood prominently before the country as the champion of responsible administration :

> " And moving up from high to higher,
>   Became, on fortune's crowning slope,
>   The pillar of a people's hope."

* Political Notes. By G. E. Fenety, Esq.

In the meantime, however, the Opposition was formidable and the battle was furious. All the scattered forces of the old Conservative system, marshalled with consummate skill, were gathered into most determined opposition. The adherents of opposite standards resolutely maintained the struggle and fiercely contended for victory. For the reform party the contest apparently proved to be a most disastrous one. In a House of Assembly of forty-one members, the only representatives of that principle were Messrs. Wilmot and Fisher. In Fredericton the poll was for a time threatened by a rough, lawless, and unfranchised crowd. For the protection of voters, and the prevention of organized intimidation, it was found expedient to call out the military. In double file the soldiers were stationed with fixed bayonets. Each of the later voters, for personal security, accompanied by a sergeant, between lines of glittering steel, passed up to the poll and gave his suffrage. At the close, Mr. Wilmot, amongst the successful candidates, unrolled a scarlet silk flag bearing the significant motto *Responsible Government.* Through Queen Street, from the old Court House to a platform near Phœnix Square, he was carried by his enthusiastic supporters; and, amidst deafening cheers, made a splendid and stirring speech. The banner thus exultingly unfurled, borne in triumphal procession and the proud signal of victory, at the close of that struggle, through all the liberal ranks, was the only one which told of success. There had been everywhere, for reform, signal defeat and sore

disaster; and, over the entire field, their banners
trailed sadly in the dust. The party of progress, for
the time, was thoroughly and terribly routed and
shattered. But there was still a great principle in
contention and a noble cause around which they could
rally their scattered forces. Temporary disadvantage
they might be doomed to experience. But, in the end,
their principles, guaranteed by the spirit of British
constitutional liberty, were certain to prevail : for

> "Freedom's battle, once begun,
>   Bequeathed by bleeding sire to son,
>   Though baffled oft, is ever won."

"Looking back along the line of those years, we
seem to be gazing into the crater of an extinct volcano.
The inflammable matter which fed the fire of debate,
and the fury with which each step of political progress
was discussed by the great antagonists on either side,
has been so bitterly burned out and extinguished, that
we in this generation, who dwell on the fertile soil of
social and religious freedom formed by those con-
vulsions, can scarcely believe in the bitterness of the
struggle and the ability and boldness of the statesmen
by whom each prize of our present liberties was
won."

In 1844, as a slight tribute to the progress of liberal
ideas, Mr. Wilmot was appointed a member of the
Executive; but, disapproving of Sir William Cole-
brooke's impolitic and arbitrary action in the appointment of his son-in-law, Mr. Reade, to an important
Government office, involving direct violation of a vital

principle and contention, and deemed subversive of representative responsibility, that position was soon after resigned. "It would be vain," said Hon. Mr. Wilmot, in written explanation, required by the Governor, of reasons for tendering his resignation as a member of the Executive Council, "for the parents of youth to make every exertion in order to qualify their sons for the higher offices of the Province, if the avenues to honourable and profitable preferment are to be closed against them ; and I therefore cannot but view the appointment under consideration as an act of great injustice to the people of this country, and I can safely assure your Excellency that it will be thus considered throughout the length and breadth of the Province."

In the political world, as in every domain of free thought and of unshackled action, extremes must sometimes meet. In resistance of prerogative, Mr. Wilmot was thrown to the utmost point of opposition: "the Government would henceforth be taught to know, and the cry would go forth from the Gulf Shore to the Scoodic, that the people would have their rights." But in an opposite direction, as pole from pole, his sense of political justice was subjected to severe strain. For the first time in party vote, while holding port-folio in 1844, he was separated from usual political associates. They proposed to censure the government, because in recent appointments to the Legislative Council, the proportionate claims of the several denominations had been over-

looked. They were for the policy of many State
Churches. He was for none. Chivalrously, and at
the risk of alienated sympathy, he contended for
broad and generous catholicity of spirit and action.
The rights of "fellow-dissenters" he would conserve,
and to the utmost advocate ; but to the perpetuation
of religious tests, under any conditions, he was utterly
opposed. " The narrow rule of selection, from this or
that denomination," was denounced. He advocated
" the more expansive policy which, regardless of all
religious differences, selects men best fitted by integrity, ability, and property, to represent the whole
people."

After twelve years of costly and almost incessant
warfare, with varied and alternating fortunes, pending
the General Election of 1846, Mr. Wilmot resolved
upon retirement from political life.

Though, in the first place, in 1834, his seat in the
House of Assembly was obtained by acclamation ; yet,
subsequently, in no less than five general elections, he
had abundant experience of the inconvenience, expenditure, fearful excitement, and frequent lawlessness
which at that time were the inseparable concomitants
of an election campaign. Under the vicious system
which then prevailed, the poll was kept up for eight
days. There was an open vote. Aroused by partizan
and inflammatory speeches, the several constituencies
had ample license and opportunity for excess and explosion. The agitation through all these days swept
over the country, deepened in its course, and not un-

frequently ended in turbulence and almost riot. In some respects the eloquent and liberal member for York was not eminently qualified for a contest of that nature. For a temperament such as his the excitement was too intense. In the severe attrition of opposite forces, and the fierce collision of adverse factions, the impetuous and combustible elements of composition and mental constitution, with which he was abundantly charged, blazed out into white heat; and, in brilliant, impassioned, most vehement speech, streamed forth in a lava-like torrent.

It cannot be wondered at that a keenly-sensitive and high-toned mind, though eminently qualified for parliamentary debate, and delighting in the discussion of constitutional questions, should recoil from the shock and severity of hustings' warfare. In view of the next approaching dissolution of the House, to the general regret of nearly all political parties, by whom his superb rhetoric and chivalrous bearing were greatly admired, he announced his intention to withdraw from the Legislature. That purpose, however, he was not then suffered to consummate. By the enthusiasm and organization of friends and party, without personal canvass or campaign, he was proudly and triumphantly returned for the old constituency. The star of reform was now in the ascendency.

Through years of conflict, embittered by contempt of the governing class, impelled by conviction of pressing necessity for constitutional change, and the introduction into the system of Colonial government of

c

elements compatible with fair and equitable administration, Mr. Wilmot and his coadjutors had struggled
on to ultimate and decisive success.* The "compact"
monopoly was swept away, and the despotism of
oligarchy demolished. Responsible government was
fully inaugurated, and the principle of Ministerial
accountability, long the accepted basis of British administration, was adopted as the solution of difficulties
between the executive and representative departments
of Government. Instead of permanent official appointments, advisers of the Crown were to be selected from
the party at the time in the ascendency ; and provision
was made for obtaining the sanction of constituencies
to all departmental appointments. To all positions of
honor and emolument, without regard to class or creed,
and free from social restrictions, the avenues were
fully opened.

A Government was organized for the purpose of
giving effect to responsible policy. It comprised a
large and influential Conservative element ; and, in the
matter of arrangements, there was necessity for compromise. But, in regard to the main principle, the colors
were never lowered. "He could not forget the election

* Through all this contest, calculated, as in a crucible, to try the
mettle and the mould of men, as an able tactician, capable of flank
movement—an adept in the manipulation of resolutions, and a competent exponent of great constitutional principles, Mr. Wilmot found
an able and accomplished colleague in Mr. Chas. Fisher, now Judge of
the Supreme Court. On the 24th February, 1848, he moved the resolution which, by admission of all parties, unequivocally committed the
country to the principles of Responsible Government.

of 1842," he said, in one of his great speeches in the House of Assembly, "when responsible government was scouted, jeered at, and held up to ridicule over the length and breadth of the land. But a different day had dawned upon the Province. The people had informed themselves—had begun to see and understand and appreciate those glorious principles—the principles of the British Constitution—not his principles alone; they were the principles of every British subject. He was a mere machine in working out the great system; but those great and glorious principles would live when those who heard his voice were laid low in the dust. Those principles were not intended for the exclusive benefit of one class, or one party, or one family; but for the benefit of every class, of every party, and of every family over the length and breadth of the land. Responsible government held out even-handed justice and fair play to all. He had put on the uniform when it was covered with obloquy, and had worn it amidst scoutings and jeers, and felt proud to bear it now."*

An element of offensive Conservatism, conspicuous in government, had also been inwrought into the structure and administration of Education. It was a favorite theory of Mr. Wilmot that, instead of ascent from the primary to the academic, the current of educational life-force descends from the University; and, through all grades and departments, makes its influence felt and determines the status of the system. The College

* Political Notes. By G. E. Fenety, Esq.

at Fredericton, though liberally endowed and favored
with an efficient staff of Professors, was for many years
unpopular; and in 1844 it was asserted in the Legislature that the sum expended upon it, up to that time,
"would have educated every one of the students at
Oxford or Cambridge." It was in a very considerable
measure owing to his efforts and advocacy that, with
constitution modified, a representation of the several
leading denominations upon its Senate, and general
administration popularized, the Provincial University
has entered upon a course of acknowledged efficiency
and of increasing prosperity.

In an able and exhaustive speech, when *first* the
measure for reform was proposed—the question was
repeatedly brought up until 1845, when an amended
charter passed into law—and in a calm, moderate, states-
manlike spirit and style, he traced out and earnestly
deprecated the existence of a variety of invidious distinctions, chiefly of a religious nature, which the
original charter had created, and which had tended to
excite hostility to the College and to impair its usefulness. It was proposed for supervision to substitute
the Governor for the Bishop; to annul a provision of
the charter to the effect that the President must be an
Episcopal clergyman, and *ex-officio* the Archdeacon; to
liberalize the Constitution of the College Council; to
abolish religious tests, except in regard to the Professor
of Theology; for subscription to the Thirty-Nine
Articles of the Church of England, to require from
graduates a profession of belief in "the authenticity

and divine inspiration of the Old and New Testaments and in the doctrine of the Trinity."*

The cause of public education was deeply rooted in Mr. Wilmot's sympathies. He believed in this boon as the birthright of every New Brunswick child; and, on the part of parents, deplored the apathy existing in some parts of the country. In a community of his own county a promise had been made that, if the people would get out the frame for a school-house, the expense of other necessary material for its completion should be provided for them. But, "although boards were offered from a neighbouring mill, nails, glass, locks, latches—everything without money—no one felt interest enough in the education of their children to bring them to the spot. To this day that frame stands a melancholy monument of dreadful apathy." To meet such neglect, and to rescue the children of the soil from threatened degradation, it was proposed to assess the property of the country. Far in advance of the time for the incipiency of such a policy, in the House of Assembly, the honourable member for York moved a resolution to the effect: *"The man who has property and no children should be taxed to educate the children of the man who has no property."* There was a firm belief in the principle of a public, free, nonsectarian system. Nearly a quarter of a century later, during governmental administration, it was a cause of proud and grateful satisfaction that a com-

Vide Observer, January, 1839.

prehensive educational scheme should be successfully
inaugurated.*

In a parliamentary debate, March, 1847, on L. A.
Wilmot's motion in relation to "School Reserve," the
educational question was again brought to the front.
Early in the settlement of the country there had been
an extensive *reserve* of public lands "for the use of
parish schools in the different counties." The Government was challenged "with having granted large quan-
tities of lands," originally reserved for the endowment
of public education, amounting to upwards of six
thousand acres, to the Churches of England and Scot-
land. It was charged that Government had no more
right to interfere with these lands than to touch the
Bank of England. It was alleged that in one day
Government had granted several thousand acres of
these lands to the English Church, in trust to the Chief-
Justice, the Archdeacon, the Attorney and Solicitor
Generals, and other public officers, to be used as
churches should be built."†

In the revolution which was now to be speedily
effected, this arrangement led to a curious anomaly.
As the result of successful advocacy of liberal principles, Mr. W. was called upon to form a Government.
In that administration he accepted an office which,
like most good things in those days, had been regarded

---

* To the statesmanship of Hon. Geo. E. King mainly belongs the
credit of formulating the educational system of New Brunswick, and
of carrying it into law.

† Political Notes, page 256.

as peculiarly an Episcopal preserve. It had not been supposed that there would soon dawn a day in which a gifted "dissenter" would be regarded as eligible for such honourable appointment. For the possible contingency there had been no provision made. The consequence was that, *ex-officio*, there was a trust of extensive glebe lands to be administered for the benefit of the Church of England. It was not too soon, in the public interest, that the hour had come and the man for a free ventilation of wholesale and insufferable monopoly.

Ardent as was the loyalty of L. A. Wilmot, and especially susceptible of popular influence, it was always under the restraint and control of prudential and economic considerations. The disbursement of public moneys was felt to be a responsibility and trust. In opposition to a movement, in 1846, for a legislative grant in aid of individual subscription for the erection of a monument in the city of St. John, somewhat in the style of Bunker Hill of Boston, in commemoration of the landing of the Loyalists in 1783, now nearly a century ago, he said: "There was no doubt but that this was a fine subject for a speech ; but, as a descendant of an old Loyalist, he felt himself degraded by the begging attitude assumed in this appeal for a Provincial grant. New Brunswick needed no brass—no marble—to commemorate the landing of that noble, devoted band ; their memories would be handed down to posterity without the aid of monuments or of obelisks."

The activity and assured confidence of Mr. Wilmot, to which the eagerness and enthusiasm of his constituents—throughout the triumphant election campaign of 1846—had communicated the impulse of renewed energy, and the comprehensiveness of his proposed scheme of reform, may be inferred from current correspondence. Having been urged to become a candidate for the Speakership in the House of Assembly for 1847, breathing the genuine spirit of a patriot statesman, he wrote: " As I believe 'there is a Providence that shapes our ends, rough-hew them as we will,' so I begin to think that if the Chair were at my command, I should hesitate before I took my seat. I see many momentous questions involving the present and future prosperity of this Province, and the North American Colonies generally, wherein I should like to take an active part: Confederation of all the North American Colonies—establishment of a pure Free Trade between the Colonies and the Mother Country —thorough reform in our Parish Schools—comprehensive and practicable Schemes for the allotment and occupation of our wilderness lands by a superior class of Immigrants—hand-to-hand fight against our corrupt system of appropriating the Public Revenue until it is exterminated, or rather eradicated.

" These and other questions of less moment are fraught with incalculable advantages, if rightly disposed of. To bring about the two first *would be worth the expenditure of what little of life I have remaining, and the lives of a score of better men.* What shall I do ?

I want to be free to act, and to act with all my energies
on these questions, and I fear the Chair would be a
dead weight upon me—and if so, I want no dead
weight.   We must give up our lives for the conflict.
It will be *principle* against *prejudice*, *purity* against
corruption, *greatness* against *littleness*, *light* against
darkness, *British glory* against *Bluenose tinsel*, the
sun against a *rush light*—and yet true as are these
antithetic descriptions, there will be found those who
will make a desperate defence for the corruption, the
littleness, the darkness, &c., and who will tell us the
country will be ruined by their accomplishment."

The ideal of Mr. Wilmot, in regard to commercial
policy and tariff arrangements, which at the present
time have been thrown to the front and challenge the
most prominent consideration, seems to have been :
Free Trade between Great Britain and her dependen-
cies, also between the several Colonies ; and, in relation
to other countries, a discriminating system of protection.   The essential conditions of national policy since
then, of course, have been completely changed.   We
cannot now complain that any pent-up Utica contracts
our powers.   But, at a period when even the trade of
sister Colonies was hampered by custom duties, it was
felt that any available market must, to a considerable
extent, be bounded by the limits of the Province.
" These duties," said the honourable member for York,
during the *revenue* discussion of 1847, in a characteristic speech, " were in fact a disgrace to the Colonies.
What was the case in the United States ?   They could
C*

learn a useful lesson there. There was no such re-
striction; they had the whole American world for a
market. The shoemaker at Lynn could go where he
pleased, from Maine to New Orleans. But New
Brunswick rivalled all the world beside! Where was
our market? At home—cramped up in a narrow
little Province containing about 150,000 inhabitants.
The humble mechanic with a lapstone on his knee had
a mind—an intellect; but, so long as he had no market
beyond the bounds of his own narrow Province, he
would remain stationary. But tell him that the whole
British world is before him, and you set his mind to
work. Those wholesome regulations of the United
States had brought out the mind—the genius—the
extraordinary genius of that people. Little countries
made little mechanics and little statesmen. Look at
the extraordinary list of inventions for which patents
have been granted to the State of Massachusetts
alone. In this way the latent energies of mind were
brought into action. *He regretted that any restrictions had ever been placed upon Intercolonial
trade.*"

There was another important movement, then growing up into formidable organization, and which now
challenges still more commanding recognition, that
made its voice to be heard within the halls of the New
Brunswick Legislature. In 1847, in consequence of a
motion for a grant in aid of the St. John *Temperance
Telegraph,* eloquently and successfully advocated by
Mr. Wilmot, the Temperance question came up in the

Assembly for a full and exhaustive discussion. This debate, the first probably of a series, deserves prominence in the annals of Colonial legislation. The subject is doubtless destined to continued discussion in Parliament, through the press, and on the platform, until its principles shall have thoroughly permeated the nation; and the dark blot of legislation, which sanctions and legalizes the unhallowed liquor traffic, with all the enormity of evil, of crime, pauperism and perdition, that follow in its course, shall have been removed from the Statute Book of this professedly Christian country; and when, through all these lands, the banner of Temperance shall wave in uncontested triumph.

In our times the public press has become a potent political engine, the tongue of a free people, and a stupendous social influence. The columns of enterprising and leading newspapers contain and circulate much of the best thought and ablest composition of the time; and, in the ventilation of public questions, they form a most convenient medium of access to the popular mind. During the most active period of L. A. Wilmot's career, the present era of influential journalism, comparatively, was at its commencement. But even then it was an agency not to be neglected. Strange does it seem, as we are nearing to the close of the century, that, within the memory of recent events, this fact of occasional contribution should call for explanation and vindication: "He would not deny that he had written for the papers—some little squibs.

Did not the first noblemen and statesmen in England write for the papers ?" *

In May, 1848, the Hon. L. A. Wilmot was appointed to the office of Attorney-General. The duties which, as Leader of the House of Assembly and Premier of the Province, in the administration of government and the manipulation of measures, now devolved upon him, open a new chapter of political history. They were of a nature to demand constructive ability and the exercise of another kind of power from that by which he had been thrown to the front of opposition. From several measures of great utility, shadowed forth in the Attorney-General's scheme of government, including railway extension, reciprocity, consolidation of law, agriculture and education, it would not be easy to form any adequate estimate of his executive ability. There was no clear field for statesmanship. The period of his administration was one of transition. There had been departure from old lines of action ; but the course for the future had yet to be clearly and definitely ascertained and determined. The adaptation and adjustment of Government functions to new and altered conditions and circumstances very fully occupied the time and thought of the Assembly. There was but a scanty margin left for the discussion of economic measures.

One of the first questions demanding attention was that of salaries. Under a system of monopoly, the scale of payment, official and judicial, had been high in

* Want of Confidence Debate, 1847.

proportion to the resources of the Province. There was expectation of immediate retrenchment. But there were also, as a disturbing and confusing element, the claim and complication of vested right. A delicate and dexterous hand was required to draw a distinct and satisfactory line of mediation between Conservative and Liberal section and sentiment, and equally and evenly to protect and promote individual and provincial interests. " He was at present," said the leader of responsible administration, " a member of Government, yet he felt himself unchanged in regard to high salaries. He had witnessed from his youth up the evil effects of them in this community, when those in more humble life attempted to imitate the habits and manners of the official ; but the Government did not pay a man to roll about in splendor in his carriage, and give *fetes* and balls : they expected him to use his mental faculties, and to receive the benefit of his mind." *

In 1849, the Attorney-General, Hon. L. A. Wilmot, in anticipation of a scheme for several years postponed —the construction of a railroad from Halifax to Quebec—carried a measure through the House pledging

---

* " I am willing not only to admit, but even anxious to assert, that in fixing the amount of official salaries in British North America, great frugality should be observed. In countries recently settled it is of moment that moderate and simple habits of domestic expenditure should prevail, and should be respected ; nor is there any exception to that rule which I should more strongly deprecate than one which would enable, if not require, official men to distinguish themselves from other classes by a less strict economy and a more costly style of life."—*Lord Glenelg.*

a grant of certain public lands and the revenue of the
Province to the extent of £20,000 annually for twenty
years. In common with many others, whose specula-
tions could not at that time be brought to the crucial
test of actual fact, when the question of local roads
was mooted, and the balance of direct expenditure and
of indirect advantage of traffic and travel were not
well understood, he was quite sceptical in regard to the
development of a trade that would warrant the immense cost involved. In mingled banter and sarcasm,
he characterized the first proposed scheme of railway
as "a line from St. John to Shediac"—cut out by the
Colonial Minister and renewed by the emigrant agent
—"built for the purpose of transporting salt from
Westmoreland, oysters from Shediac, Cumberland
butter, and Tantramar hay." The prevalent idea at
that time was: local traffic would financially be insig-
nificant; and, in order to benefit extensively by railway thoroughfares, they must open communication
with distant and populous centres.

As representative of the Province of New Brunswick, in 1850, Mr. Attorney-General Wilmot attended
the International Railway Convention at Portland, in
the State of Maine. The occasion was one of more
than ordinary interest. It was the first time since
Bunker Hill, for the promotion of beneficent and
national projects, that sons of Loyalists and Revolu-
tionists had met in fraternal intercourse. *The flags of
the two countries were interwoven.* The Convention
was summoned on that last July day for the purpose

of considering the feasibility, by rail *via* New Brunswick, of connecting the cities of Halifax and Portland.

Into the magnificent schemes projected at Portland he threw himself with all the enthusiastic impulse of his nature. He was not always in a mood, owing possibly to hereditary Loyalist prejudice and educational bias, to do justice to the men and the measures of the American Republic. Statesmen, having in charge great destinies, were not believed to have clean hands; presidential elections were likely to produce serious disturbance; the great West, the safety valve, would fill up, and then the Union would be subjected to its severest strain. But, at the Convention, international themes were to the front: the common heritage of the conquering Saxon race—the advantages of international comity—the era, now beginning to dawn, of greatly-increased inter-communication—the splendid developments of an unfettered commerce—the banners of the Republic and of the Empire: the starry folds of the Union, emblematical of God's great works in creation, and the red-cross flag of England, of greater work in Redemption, waving in undisturbed harmony—

> " Till the war-drum throbbed no longer,
> And the battle-flags were furled
> In the Parliament of man, the
> Federation of the world."

Between the British Colonies and the United States there was a natural, geographical, and commercial interdependence. In the name of concord and mutual

welfare and prosperity, he proclaimed a bond of indis-
soluble union between the two countries. By means
of the iron rail, their possessions, broad as the Conti-
nent, would be linked together; and, like the wedding
ring, the symbol of plighted faith, it would constitute
a guarantee of permanence. Under that ban he pealed
anathema upon the restless demagogues of either land
who should seek to part them asunder.

" He alluded to the fact that exercise of the muscles
of the body tended to increased vigor ; and that exercise
of intellectual faculties, and interchange of opinions,
strengthened the mind. Reciprocity of kindly feeling
would, in like manner, enlarge the heart. In the
course of his remarks, Mr. Wilmot casually alluded to
the question of *dissolution* of the Union—that the
people of the Provinces would look upon such an event
as most disastrous to their interests and to the interests
of humanity. He thought that even a suggestion in
that direction ought to be considered treason by law ;
and, with much earnestness, exclaimed : '*Perish the
man who should dare to think of it.*' " *

There were many able and eloquent speeches at that
Portland Convention, from parliamentary and public
men—both sides of the line—but to Attorney-General
Wilmot, by common consent, was awarded the palm of
consummate, crowning oratory. He carried the audience by storm. To people across the border, accustomed to political declamation, it was a matter of
amazement that their most brilliant men should be

* Portland *Advertiser.*

completely eclipsed. It was still a greater cause of mystery how a style of oratory, of the imaginative and impassioned type, regarded as peculiarly a production of the chivalrous and sunny South, could have been born and nurtured amidst the frigid influences and monarchical institutions of a bleak and foggy forest Province. There were accompanying advantages which stamped the effort as supreme of its kind. Dramatic action, consummate grace of rhetorical expression, a voice of matchless power and wondrous modulation, contributed to the heightened effect. To a very considerable extent the eloquence was impromptu; and, therefore, largely took its caste and complexion, apt allusions and rich surprises, from the immediate scene and its surroundings. That magnificent burst of oratory swept over the audience like fire amongst stubble, and like the tempest that bends forest trees. Reporters are said to have dropped their pencils and yielded to the magnetic, resistless spell; and the people, gathered in dense mass, were wrought into a frenzy of excitement and enthusiasm. It was very importunately desired that upon public, social, and international themes, he would make a round of speeches in the chief centres of the Union.

"I am poor," said a Revolutionary hero, a century ago, when tempted by a bribe of British gold; "but the King of Great Britain, with all the treasures of his exchequer, is not rich enough to buy me." Time works its own revenges. "What is your price?" demanded a knot of wealthy Republicans, believing in the Sir

Robert Walpole doctrine. "My price!" said the Hon.
L. A. Wilmot; "what is it that you mean?" "Every
man has a price," it was affirmed, "and you have only
to name yours and you shall have it." And thus the
eloquent Attorney-General of the little Province by the
sea, had he been accessible on that side, might, as he
afterwards phrased it, have been "turned into a
Republican stump orator." But he had the stern stuff
of that hero of the Revolution; and, without bravado,
could have told of another land that held his heart, and
of a nobler mission:

> "To struggle in the solid ranks of truth;
> To clutch the monster error by the throat;
> To bear opinion to a loftier seat,
> To blot the era of oppression out,
> And lead a new and nobler freedom in."

During the same year, 1850, Attorney-General
Wilmot visited Washington. Negotiations, in which
his Government was concerned, had been opened for a
Treaty of Reciprocity with the United States; but for
the maturity of such a scheme, time was demanded.
Four years later, through the agency of Lord Elgin,
the project was happily consummated.

III.

JUDGE AND GOVERNOR.

"Sans peur et sans reproche."
—Mémoires, &c.

N January, 1851, Hon. L. A. Wilmot was appointed Judge of the Supreme Court. It was as Judge that, in a large circle, he is now remembered and venerated. The Chief-Justiceship, then vacant, following the analogy of the British Constitution, was due to him as Attorney-General. Through Conservative influence, endeavouring to thwart responsible administration, and the persistency of the Governor, this more exalted seat was given to Mr. Justice Carter. The Puisne Judgeship offered to Mr. Wilmot, contrary to general expectation, was accepted. By many of his political friends this step was regarded as the mistake of his life. It was the opinion of competent counsellors that he should have protested against the elevation of Judge Carter, and gone into opposition. There was every reason to believe, that

by such a course, he might have consolidated the
Reform Party, foiled the schemes of Sir E. Head, upset
the Conservative Government; and, that being made
acquainted with manifest violation of constitutional
principle, in the end the Colonial Minister would have
given him the position in contention.

The annals of British judicial administration, from
the days of Sir Matthew Hale, "for deep discernment
praised" and "sanctity undefiled," through a golden
age of law and reason, a long and splendid succession,
commemorate the names of distinguished Judges;
their supreme legal attainments and conspicuous
mental endowments constitute a pride and glory of the
realm.   Under pressure of counter and conflicting
claims and considerations, at the time of the Judge's
appointment, to the perplexity of friends and a provo-
cation to adverse criticism, there was somewhat of
hesitation and perhaps of oscillation betwixt the
Forum and the Bench. He was a popular politician.
The House of Assembly had been the scene of magnificent oratorical achievement. But then he was also
a _lawyer_—passionately proud of his profession and
conscious of competent qualification for discharge of
onerous and exalted duty. In deference, therefore, to
special attraction and the unrivalled _prestige_ of dignified legal position, ardent and enthusiastic sympathies
and aspirations were placed in subordination. He was
still in the meridian splendour of public life. But the
preference was laudable and perfectly explicable. He
had his reward. The ambition, which as the crown

and culmination of a brilliant and influential career—professional and parliamentary—coveted honourable and illustrious association and a place on the bead-roll of immortal forensic fame, was well calculated to ensure and perpetuate recognition.

In addition to reasons already indicated, that determined his course, there were probably others of a private and personal nature. As a consequence of early entrance upon public life, his own business must have been greatly neglected; and professional income, upon which he was mainly dependent, would be considerably curtailed. The inevitable cost of contested elections, under the vicious system which at that time prevailed, must under any circumstance have been a very serious item. In these facts there was palpable and cogent reason for accepting honourable judicial appointment—a coveted prize in the legal profession. The transition from stormy debates of the Legislative Assembly to the ordinarily serene atmosphere of the Court of Judicature, not altogether consonant to mercurial elements of mental temperament, brought with it duties of an entirely different character. He was now largely withdrawn from the public gaze. For some seventeen years, in the impartial discharge of judicial functions, he stood aloof from party movement. This phase of life may, therefore, fitly be compressed into *brief* notice.

To the Bench of New Brunswick Judge Wilmot became a noble and splendid accession. He was not by any means a *black-letter* lawyer. At the bar, in the

shape of ancient and musty authorities, he never bored
judge or jury by any extra production of learned
lumber. There is a kind of legal knowledge to be obtained in patient, labourious inquiry and application,
for which he would never, probably, have become conspicuous. As a mere *legist* of what may be technically
known as "cases," from the fibre and constitution of
his mind, he could scarcely have achieved any signal
success. In contradistinction to a dull plodder in
precedent, he was pre-eminently a jurist. "Under any
species of administration," according to the dictum of
a distinguished aphorist, "it is seldom that both intellect and intregity have a predominating sway."
But in a very eminent degree and in marked combination, when Mr. Justice Wilmot presided at the Supreme
Court, these desiderated qualities found exhibition.
Keen observation, love for legal studies, extensive professional experience, acute and penetrating thought,
clear and facile intuition and perception of complex
and subtle questions involved, firm and rapid grasp of
principles that govern the noble science of jurispru-
dence, in that lofty sphere, could not fail to command
appreciation and profound respect. That very rapidity
and assurance of mental process, however, by which
complicated interests and important issues were appre-
hended and anticipated, were almost certain in some
cases to produce friction and dissatisfied feeling.
Between the Bench and Bar may often be felt the
pressure of motives that lie widely asunder. There is
ample margin for divergence of feeling and action. The

persistence of the advocate, knowing how much has
been staked upon his ability and judgment, and what
important interests have been entrusted to his management, sometimes deemed sheer pertinacity, striving to
make the worse appear the better cause, is not unfrequently prompted by intense and anxious solicitude
for the advantage of a client. The Judge on the other
hand has only one central, controlling idea. He strives
to be absolutely and inflexibly impartial. Through
whatever human hopes, fears, or supposed rights, it
cleave a way, the law must take its course. Upon
whatever tends to thwart pure administration, justice
sternly frowns rebuke. Occasionally impatience, provoked by the wrangling of lawyers, finds severe expression. But whatever difference of estimate there may
have been in regard to Judge Wilmot's administration,
in other respects, there was confessedly an unswerving
integrity of purpose. In his appointment to the Bench
the ermine was worn with dignity, grace, and unsullied
purity.

One trial during his presidency as Judge of the
Supreme Court, amongst scientific men and through
the country, is said to have excited a deep and widespread interest. Amongst the witnesses summoned
were Professor Sedgewick, the noted geologist, and
eminent scientists of the United States. The issue of
the trial depended chiefly upon correct classification of
a mineral, a species of anthracite extensively used in
the manufacture of kerosene oil, commonly known as
Albert coal. Testimony in this case, for purposes of

accuracy, comprised some very minute distinctions and abundance of technical terminology. The Judge was now in his element. Wide and varied knowledge, legal and scientific, was exhibited to very conspicuous advantage. He gave himself to thorough mastery and complete comprehension of the questions in disputation. The ability with which he presided, the luminous exposition of fundamental principles of law, the acuteness exhibited in grasp of multifarious details and scientific intricacies, commanded general admiration. From intelligent spectators and distinguished witnesses, most competent to determine, he won acknowledgment of the highest encomium.

The value to his country for many years' service, in faithful discharge of judicial duties, consonant with the pure and lofty spirit of the British legal administration, from a mere reference to isolated cases, cannot be fully estimated. "The pure and impartial administration of justice is, probably, the firmest bond to secure a cheerful submission of the people, and to engage their affections to government." * "Justice is the greatest interest of man on earth. It is the ligament which holds civilized beings and civilized nations together. Wherever her temple stands, and as long as it is duly honoured, there is a foundation for security, and general happiness, and the improvement and progress of our race. And whoever labours on this edifice with usefulness and distinction ; whoever clears its foundations, strengthens its pillars, adorns its entabla-

* *Letters of Junius.*

tures, or contributes to raise its august dome still higher in the skies, connects himself, in name and fame and character, with that which is and must be durable as human society." *

During the period of connection with the Bench a relief from severe strain of judicial duty, in response to pressing application, taking advantage of convenient and legitimate method of acting upon popular thought and feeling, Judge Wilmot occasionally lectured on subjects of literary and patriotic interest. Toward the close of the Crimean War, in 1856, a second address on that subject was delivered. The theme was congenial. After much endurance, and one of the greatest sieges on record, the fortressed City of Sebastopol had been taken. The haughty pride and menace of Russia were laid in the dust. In discussing the situation there were accuracy of detail, precision of technical and military phrase, and vividness of colouring that would have done credit to one who had mingled in the strife. There was a very decided impression that the best interests of a noble civilization, and of a nobler christianity, were bound up with the success of the Allies. Believing that God was still " the Lord of Hosts "—the Supreme Arbiter of nations—he referred, for patriotic purpose, to sacred historic fact and to the might of ancient Hebrew warriors. Full of the fire of that theme, on the destruction of Sennacherib's host, he quoted Byron's Hebrew melody :

* *Daniel Webster.*

D

" The Assyrian came down, like the wolf on the fold,
   And his cohorts were gleaming in purple and gold ;
   And the sheen of their spears was like the stars on the sea,
   When the blue wave rolls nightly on deep Galilee."

During the troubled days of the Sepoy mutiny, in India, the march of the gallant Havelock was graphically described. Even the dark clouds which at the time gathered over our countrymen in that land had a fringe of brightness. "It was not for him to investigate the secrets of Providence ; but there seemed to be wonderful adaptations in relation to these late events." It was a happy circumstance that the rebellion in India had not happened two years earlier; then England was engaged in war with Russia. Had this been the case, every European must have died, or been driven into the sea. But again a dispute had taken place with China ; a large number of soldiers were out on the way for the purpose of settling that dispute. The Chinese contingent was, therefore, ready to enter India just when the terrible outbreak happened.

A series of Lyceum addresses, in the city of St. John, 1858-9, grew into fame. The audiences and excitement were unprecedented in that community. The design of the whole course was to deepen in the public mind a sense of indebtedness to the Word of God. Many a thread of purple and gold was woven into the texture of brilliant speech. The touching testimony of Dr. Newman, in regard to " the uncom-
-mon beauty and marvellous" style of the authorized

version, was emphasized and endorsed: " It lives in the ear like music that can never be forgotten, like the sound of the church bells which the convert hardly knows how to forego. Its felicities seem almost things instead of words ; it is a part of the national mind and the anchor of national seriousness; the memory of the dead passes into it; the potent traditions of childhood are stereotyped in its verses; the power of all griefs and trials of man are hidden beneath its words. In the length and breadth of the land there is not a Protestant, with one spark of seriousness about him, whose spiritual biography is not in the Saxon Bible."[*]

Amongst the generous gifts of a loyal people to the Princess Royal, on the occasion of her marriage to the Crown-Prince of Prussia, was a superbly bound Bible, " the secret of England's greatness "—

> " A gem which purer lustre flings
> Than the diamond flash of the jewelled crown
> On the lofty brow of kings."

In reference to that gift, " a boon offered alike to prince and to peasant," the Judge paid a beautiful tribute to the Book he loved so well: " There were gathered in profusion, costly pearls and diamonds, brilliant, dazzling ornaments, precious gifts from loving friends. One would think that art had exhausted its skill in producing those wondrous bridal gifts ; and one is led to think how they will adorn England's daughter, and how these precious gems will ere long

* Dublin *Review.*

sparkle in the light of a thousand lamps in the royal
halls of Prussia. And then those mementoes of
domestic love, how they will remind her of the generous givers and of her happy English home! But see!
amid that costly, dazzling array there is another gift.
It cannot deck the brow, or sparkle on the bosom; but
it can do more, infinitely more. When pearls, and
diamonds, and gems, and gold and gay attire, lose all
their beauty and attraction; when all worldly glories
are fading away, this precious gift will only increase
in value and in beauty, reflecting the light of heaven
upon the soul, and affording sweet peace when all of
earth is useless, valueless. Here are decorations for
the soul, brilliants for eternity!"

The pure and life-giving Word of God was designed,
as the lecturer believed, for nations as well as individuals. The inspired idea of the mystic river of prophetic vision, on more than one occasion, found noble
application: "I like," he said, at the St. John
Anniversary of 1858, "to refer to that striking
vision of the prophet Ezekiel in the 47th chapter,
where he sees the great waters stretching away,
far away: It is like the Word of God; and there
we see the little Sunday-school children coming
up, and it is ankle-deep for them; and then we
see it growing deeper and broader for those more
advanced in years, the waters coming up to the knees,
and then the loins, until it swelled out a mighty river,
stretching far away, and which even the greatest could
not pass over; but some stand on the brink of this

great river of life, and will allow none to wade in it.
Some would endeavour to prevent us going into these
waters, even ankle deep, and instead of allowing us to
bathe in this glorious stream of the river of life, would
give to us but small draughts, not of the pure waters
of life, but a miserable, filthy compound, taken out of
the stagnant pools of man's devising ; or which

> Whoever tasted, lost upright shape,
> And downward fell, into a grovelling swine."

A pamphlet, published in 1859, contains a speech and
lecture, and also several controversial letters to which
these had given rise. There was an incident of the
speech that indicated breadth of historical knowledge,
and the ease with which it could at once be made
available in public effort. It had been stated by Mr.
Justice Parker, in an opening address, that Papal permission had been given in 1778 to read the Bible in
France. That permission, according to Judge Wilmot,
was for the purpose of checking the revolutionary spirit,
generated by principles and deeds that Rome had
patronized. "Voltaire and his associates were spreading their infidel writings with the avowed purpose of
overthrowing Christianity. . Copies to cover cost of
publication were sold; the remainder were gratuitous-
ly circulated. This course they commenced in 1772;
you know what happened in ten years from that time.
A living tide of fire rolled over the land, devastating
the country and sweeping before it throne and king,
altar and priest. In all this there was manifest retri-

bution and the justice of God. Two centuries before,
Clement and Ravailic, both monks, had assassinated
King Henry, excommunicated by the Pope, and Henry
of Navarre. On St. Bartholomew's Day, 1570, fifty
thousand Protestants were slaughtered. There were
rejoicings at Rome; a medal was struck in commemoration of the event. Under the pictures of Clement
and Ravailac were placed the inscription : ' Happy is
the man who kills a king.' After two hundred years,
men met in dark cells to plot the Revolution. The
pictures of Clement and Ravailac, with that inscription, were seen hanging above their heads. The king
paid the penalty. If it were good to kill Henry, why
not Louis ? Upon their own principles, the evils which
had been brought about were now avenged."

The reputation of Hon. L. A. Wilmot, as pleader
and parliamentary debater, had been made years
before; and the laurel-leaf, awarded by acclamation,
was still fresh and green. But in the absence of any
formidable opponent, a foemen worthy of keen and
polished Damascus steel, there was a general impression that the qualities which made him the Rupert of
debate must mainly be held in abeyance. There was
consequent surprise. The fire and force and freshness
of platform effort and oratory fairly took the community by storm. "For *three* hours," we find, at one
time, " the audience was held almost breathless by the
magic spell of eloquence." The announcement of John
Boyd, Esq., Hon. S. L. Tilley, Rev. Matthew Richey,
D.D., and Hon. Judge Wilmot, in 1860, as speakers

for a public meeting to be held in the Centenary Church, might well produce a feeling of more than ordinary interest. Many a great crowd has been gathered in that noble old sanctuary; but the scene of thronged aisles and galleries, that we were privileged to witness on that occasion, could scarcely be surpassed. Between two of those gifted men, it was difficult to award the palm of eloquence: "The Rev. Dr. Richey is one of the most finished orators of modern times. He would make his mark in any civilized country and among any people; his diction the purest, and his language the most chaste of any man we know. He was succeeded by Judge Wilmot in one of those thrilling, heart-stirring addresses so characteristic of him. These men are equally great in their different styles of eloquence, but they are entirely dissimilar in manner and expression. The Judge stands upon the platform a living representation of oratory." *

There was, in regard to these efforts, an almost consentaneous expression. "He lectured on the *Buried City*—of which the Prophet Nahum predicted: 'I will make thy grave, for thou art vile.' To the surprise of the wonder-stricken inhabitants; the astonishment of the world; the delight of the Bible student; the remains of this great city were discovered far below, dug out of the very bowels of the earth—a wonderful attestation of the truth of the Scripture account of Nineveh, which the sceptic has so

* *Globe.*

long derided, and of that divine prophecy uttered
many years before—'For thou hast made of a city
an heap, of a defenced city a ruin ; a place of strangers
to be no city; it shall never be built.'   Words fail
to express the rich imagery—the deep reasoning—
the wondrous development of prophecy—the solemn
lessons of warning which characterised this noble
effort.   We will only add, it was one of the richest
specimens of sublime, soul-stirring eloquence, we have
ever listened to ; and sustained, in all its force, the
fame of the speaker as one of the first orators in
America." *   For the benefit of young people the
lecture on that subject was repeated.   The hour appointed was half-past two in the afternoon ; but long
before that time the St. John Institute Hall was filled
to its utmost capacity.   "The doors had to be closed
and hundreds turned away.   The inside of the Hall
presented an imposing spectacle.   Probably not less
than two thousand five hundred managed to get in.
There were sparkling eyes and open ears.   How delightful to see his Honour devoting splendid talents to
the mental and moral improvement of the young !
Citizens are under lasting obligation for the rich intellectual treat." *   An arrangement of a similar kind
seems to have been made for the following year.
"The Christianity of the Bible," he said, "never
forged a bolt or prison bar.   It never drew a tear nor
encouraged a cruel act.   It taught peace and good-
will.   The Sword of the Spirit, the blessed Word of

* *Courier*, 1858.   † *Christian Visitor*, Feb. 1858.

God, was its only weapon. The Bible was man's heritage and right. Youthful hearers were urged to stand by it. If we may judge from the storm of applause, this they are resolved to do." *

At some points, in this memorable course, the line of thought brought up burning questions and led to the discussion of monitory historic facts. Fired by a sense of the tremendous significance of such a theme, stern as well as splendid passages burst from his lips. The fervent utterances, however, were in one case denounced as mere Protestant philippics. What was an unintentional compliment, the oratory was branded as " of the true Gavazzi style." The propriety of such a *role*, on the part of a Judge of the Supreme Court, was publicly questioned. " There was a time," he said, " when a lawyer, except as an ecclesiastic, could not sit upon the Bench. The sacred and judicial offices were combined. A chancellor heard the cause, condemned the criminal and executed the sentence." But can there be a return of such days in the history of our country ? Must the lips of legal dignitaries, except within their own jurisdiction, be utterly sealed and their convictions suppressed ? Are there not questions of momentous importance which, from eminent ability and exalted position, they are specially qualified to discuss ? Is the ermine of such delicate quality and of such sensitive purity that, by mere contact with the earnest, throbbing movements of a living humanity, it may be soiled or sullied ?

* *Church Witness*, 1859.

D*

There was at least one eminent Judge who claimed the right of untrammelled thought and of unfettered speech. His utterances in definition of position and purpose, as nobly exhibited and unfalteringly maintained, breathe and burn with the spirit and sentiment to which we are indebted for the priceless boon of civil and religious liberty. They have the ring of Luther's thundering theses : " *While under protection of the flag of my country and in possession of British freedom, I cannot allow any power or party, political or ecclesiastical, to dictate as to when, how, or where I shall explain and defend Protestant tenets and expose opposing systems.*" *

The impression produced by such words can scarcely be understood from a mere perusal. They were accompanied by an intense, but undefinable, sensibility. There was an emotion that was strangely contagious. " The Judge is all action. The listener feels his heart vibrating like a reed in the wind before his wonderful and powerful gesticulation. The oratory is that of both intellect and body ; the whole man is brought into action. Does he get off a denunciation ? You read it in his countenance before the eloquent words have leaped like fire from his lips." †

Another side of Hon. L. A. Wilmot's well-rounded life, to best advantage, could be seen in his own home. He was a versatile and brilliant conversationalist. In addition to wealth of acquired knowledge and acquaintance with best thought, as embodied in literary

* *Carleton Sentinel.* † St. John *Globe*, 1860.

art, there were ready play of wit, delicacy of feeling, love for social intercourse, and a constant atmosphere of kindliness. To bring out the interest of personal interview, it may be expedient to describe one of many visits. In order that this sketch may be a living expression, and not simply an ideal conception, it will be preferable to trace a reminiscence in which *memoranda* can be utilized.

The beautiful grounds of Evelyn Grove, at that time the finest probably in the Province, annually visited by numerous citizens and strangers, always cordially welcomed, were evidence of cultured taste and of intense love of nature.* House and verandah are draped and shaded by refreshing foliage, and beautified with thick profusion of twining plants and trellised vines. From the rear there looms up the shadowy form of dark, tall pines. Bounding the grounds are the stately and graceful forms and spreading branches of leafy greenwood trees. These have all been planted by the proprietor, and are all the growth of a life-time. Fronting the residence, intersected by pleasant paths and ornamented with statuary, smooth and velvety surface and swath of deepest and richest green, is a neatly-trimmed and shady lawn. In the midst, an appropriate setting of gem-like beauty, bright with variegated colors, is a spacious, circular mound. Geraniums and other choice plants, in various and contrasted tints, are there

* In this way, as an accomplished horticulturist, Judge Wilmot came to be widely known. He was a Vice-President of the Pomological Society of America—the President of which, the Hon. Mr. Wilder, recently paid an appropriate tribute to his memory.

combined into rare completeness and beauty of design.
In the centre, of pyramidical shape, that may only be
expected to bloom *once in a century*, stands a magnificent specimen of the cactus family. "Should the
summer-time of the hundred years come in my life,"
Judge Wilmot often pleasantly remarked, as visitors
lingered in admiration, "the church bell must ring
out a peal, and all the friends be invited to a sight of
century-flowers." That centennial glory he was not
permitted to see. The associations of that delightful
grove, in which beauty and fragrance are renewed and
reproduced, can only now revive the hopeless longing,
" O for the touch of a vanished hand, and the sound
of a voice that is still !"

Through a slender arch of bent twigs and branches,
fragrant with perfume of rose and honeysuckle and
blossoming columbine, that climb and twine around
each delicate stem, we make our way to another section of these charmingly beautiful grounds. What a
scene of floral splendour now bursts upon the view !

> " The garden paths are broad and smooth,
>   There pansies bloom in gorgeous bed ;
> And high above the violets
>   The tall, pale lilies bow their heads."

Flowers of rare beauty and loveliness, and of delicious aroma, grouped and distributed with exquisite
taste and skill, blossom and brighten in the soft balmy
sunshine ; and, with sweet odors, gladden this favored,
elysian spot. There is a sensation around you at the
moment, as if nature were sighing for repose. The

air is languid with summer heat; but in the early
morning, we should have found invigorating freshness
and the joyousness of renewed life. In matin strain,
the feathered songsters that frequent the grove warble
in concert and fill it with their melody. Here, at that
dewy hour, with wonted implements of toil, for this
floral culture forms a special charge, we might have
found our honored friend. The avenue leads at length
to another quality of production. There are superb
specimens of roots and plants, and a marvellous profusion and wealth of organic life. Threading a way
through the foliage, that almost conceals access, the
grounds in another direction change to a completely
different character. As if in some fairy land, the scene
and surroundings have undergone a wondrous trans-
formation. Instead of flowers and parenchymatous
growth, with abundance of shade, there is an almost
tropical variety of shrubbery and of thickly-planted
ornamental trees. In the centre, chiefly constructed
by his own hands, stands a summer-house of rustic
form and frame work. We find the Judge enjoying—

> " The *harvest of a quiet eye*
> That sleeps and broods on his own heart."

By the fullness and fluency of his conversation, we
are at once fascinated. The life of every plant, its
special affinities and conditions of growth, he seems
perfectly to understand. If, as the Oriental monarch,
he does not speak of the trees "from the cedar that
is in Lebanon even unto the hyssop that springeth out

of the wall;" from climbing ivy and myrtle and "the
lilies," how they grow, and fair and delicate forms of
life that have been transplanted from strange and
sunny lands, to the stately cone-bearers that tower
above us in the dusky magnificence of what seems a
dense forest growth, he talks with the accuracy of a
botanical scientist and the enthusiasm of a genuine
child of nature.

There are wonderful lessons, when once the myste-
ries of nature have found an adequate interpreter, to
be learned and treasured up. "Look," says the Judge,
"at that slender, trailing vine. In search of support,
and failing to find a fitting object, its tendrils run
along the ground. With gentle hand it ought to be
trained toward the light. There it would find strength
and life. But now, with a tendency to speedy decay,
it clasps and clings to a piece of mouldering wood. By
a law of their nature, equally with ivy plant and sum-
mer-tendril, in their unfolding mind, the little ones
that gather around us for instruction cling tenaciously
for strength and support. If not trained upwards, in
the direction of heavenly light and love, they may be
expected to take root in some unworthy object ; and,
in direct assimilation, become of the earth, earthy."
"What delicious fruit," he continues, when for a moment
the modest strawberry vine claims attention, "close
upon the surface! Is it not so in the word of God?
Are not the most essential truths easily accessible?
Were a stranger from another planet, thrown suddenly upon our globe, to be acquainted with the

boundaries of knowledge, he might ask in amazement:
' Must I know all this in order to live ? Must I search
the strata, classify planets, group the stars into con-
stellations, and investigate the illimitable'? By no
means ! The essential conditions of life are simple :
Bread from bruised corn, and water from the mountain
spring. Then, according to inclination or capacity,
research may be carried into distant domain. In the
word of God are deep abysses, mountain peaks, and
measureless expanse of thought. But the grand veri-
ties, needed for salvation, are upon the surface. *The
strawberries lie nearest to the little children !* It is not
necessary to acquire abstruse and technical knowledge
in order to live. We can subsist on that which grows
at our feet. And so in the marvellous word of inspiration, with mighty depths and knotty points for learned
men and profound theologians, for the young there are
passages, clear, simple, and loving ; the twenty-third
psalm where the little ones may be led into green
pastures and to quiet waters."

Is it the sentiment of Wordsworth, in affinity with
what has been eloquently expressed, that recurs in
suggestive strain ? As a slight contribution to con-
versational interest the lines are recalled :

> " Believe it not :
> That primal duties shine aloft like stars ;
> The charities that soothe, and heal, and bless,
> Are scattered at the feet of man like flowers."

The interest of this visit, fortunately, has not yet
ended. After an excursion through the grounds, for a

few moments of rest, we accompany the Judge to his
library. Here a new and congenial theme, often touched
upon before, is started. "Have you read," he asks—
and his words may be given *verbatim*—"the August and September numbers of Blackwood? The
first *contains* an exceedingly interesting article on *what
the Old Egyptians did*. The writer is at a loss to know
in what way the early post-diluvians became so wise
and so well instructed in many things. To me the
article is especially interesting as supporting my view
that wisdom was originally inspired by the Creator.
It does appear marvellous that even such a man as
Whately should have entertained an idea that man
when first created, or very shortly afterwards, was
advanced by the Creator himself to *a state above that of
a mere savage*. Surely if God created man perfect,
physically and morally, he did not leave him a babe in
intellect! Why may we not, therefore, assume that the
first man was educated by the Almighty Himself—
that he took the degree of M.A. in Heaven's College—
that he knew what kind of world he was placed in,
and how to make the most of it—that he knew the relation of the earth to the sun, moon and other planets,
and how they served for days and seasons and years—
that intellectually Adam was the Creator's master-piece
and never a savage? Then what opportunities, from
the longevity of the ante-diluvians, for imparting
knowledge! Though the wickedness of man was great
upon the earth, and led to the terrible judgment of the
flood, the majestic intellect was there

Bright and base,
With rubbish mixed and glittering in the dust.

The wonderful architecture of the Assyrians and Egyptians, and the learning and wisdom of the latter, necessarily indicate the transmission of a great amount of knowledge from Noah and his sons. Mankind could not in the first instance have civilized itself and must, therefore, have a superhuman instructor."

Upon the Federation of the British Colonies of North America into the Dominion of Canada, 1868, in acknowledgement of important public services not forgotten through several years of comparative seclusion, a tribute also to distinguished and commanding personal qualities, the Hon. L. A. Wilmot was appointed first native Governor of New Brunswick.* The ap-

* The first Governor of New Brunswick, for nearly twenty years, was Colonel Thomas Carleton. Then, for several years, Hon. Gabriel Ludlow and Judge Edward Winslow administered the government as Presidents. In consequence of difficulty with the United States, 1812-14, Major-General Hunter and, in rapid succession, six other officers of rank acted as military presidents. Sir George Tracy Smythe was appointed Lieutenant-Governor in 1818. Judge Chipman became administrator in 1823 and was succeeded by Hon. John Murray Bliss—uncle of L. A. Wilmot. Then, as regularly appointed Lieutenant Governors, followed Sir Howard Douglas in 1824, Sir Archibald Campbell, 1831 ; Sir John Harvey, 1834; Sir William Colebroke, 1841 ; Sir Edmund Walker Head, 1848 ; Sir J. H. Manners-Sutton, 1854 ; Sir Arthur Gordon, 1862.

Since Confederation Hon. L. A. Wilmot was succeeded by Hon., now Sir, Samuel Leonard Tilley, C.B. The brief administration of of Hon. E. B. Chandler, who followed Sir Samuel, was early terminated by death. The present Governor, Hon. R. D. Wilmot, a near relative of the Judge, completes the gubernatorial succession.

pointment was creditable to all concerned. It
could not on any side be open to the imputation of
political party purpose and manipulation. But from
disinterestedness and eminent fitness of things, no
designation could have been more politic.

The distinguished recognition accorded was purely
and pre-eminently a tribute to high character, rare
combination of mental and moral qualities, and to the
splendid services by which a reputation had been made
far beyond the boundaries of the Province. Release
from onerous judicial duties, and the comparative leisure
of governmental administration, afforded ample opportunity for literary and floral pursuits and pleasures.
What was of greater consequence an influence, always
employed for good and beneficent interests, was largely
augmented. There was also, in that appointment, an
evidence of completeness and consummation of important life work, conscious and undisguised satisfaction
and gratification. Instead of official monopoly and the
block of impassable social barriers, from the humblest
and lowliest grades and walks of life to the elevations
and altitudes of society for gifted and industrious students, the avenues were fully opened,

> "And we, in larger measure, now inherit
> What made our forerunners free and wise."

Young men, of colonial birth and education, go forth
to duty and effort; and, with all the incentive and
stimulus of possible achievement, aspire to public and
professional distinction. Let them not forget that to

Hon. L. A. Wilmot and to his compeers and compatriots, for a valuable heritage of birthright and freedom, they owe an unspeakable debt of gratitude. "Yesterday," writes a metropolitan journalist, "marked a new era in the history of New Brunswick; it marked that one of her sons, no matter of what class or creed or sect, might aspire successfully to the high dignity of becoming Lieutenant-Governor of his native Province. Sweeping away the old landmarks of vested rights and political distinction, the day has declared the lofty sentiment, that a noble genius, a loyal and patriotic spirit are the main tests of excellency, the grand desiderata of honour and distinction. In hailing Judge Wilmot as the new Lieutenant-Governor,—he comes to us with all these recommendations, traced along a whole lifetime spent in the service of his native Province; and while it is possible many of the younger portion of our people may rather incline to regard His Excellency in the light of these latter days, catching tone and feeling from recent political events, we simply ask them to look back. Let them look up the records of the past, when their grandsires were held in the grasp of domineering family compact who knew no right save the right to rule, who recognized only as presumptuous any and every aspiration of the people seeking a voice in the government of their own affairs. And when at length this Province was convulsed to its very centre, when the great Magna Charta of Responsible Government and the people's rights was struggling into existence let them ask the

'old men' who it was that sprang to the front, and
catching up this battle-cry of the people, fought the
leader in the fight until the truth and right prevailed, and won for us all that social and political
liberty which is to-day the boast of every true-born son
of New Brunswick. Nor was this merely the work
of a day. Persistently the struggle was continued from
year to year, but ever sustained by his constituents
of York, who stood by him 'in the storm and in
the sunshine,' that matchless eloquence never faltered,
that earnest, manly pleading never failed, until victory crowned the efforts of himself and colleagues,
and Responsible Government became the first principle of the constitution. Therefore it is that the
friends of His Excellency claim for him, in his recent
appointment, that he has simply obtained his right,
a right which he is worthy to receive, and *which a
vast majority of the people of his native province delight to bestow.*" *

At the inauguration of Governor Wilmot there was
a characteristic and illustrative incident that claims
permanent record. The Senate Hall on that occasion
was thronged with the *elite* of the city : ladies, sena-
tors, judges, clergymen, military gentlemen and others.
The ceremony had been completed and officials were
thronging to tender congratulation. In the excitement
of the occasion, proud of the superintendent, a little
fellow from the Sunday-school found his way to the
front. With bright intelligent face he caught the Gover-

* Fredericton *Reporter.*

nor's eye. At once, in preference to all dignitaries, the hand of the scholar was cordially grasped. No compliment could be more genuine, and certainly none was returned with more beaming light and reciprocity of feeling, than that presented by the earnest representative of his Sabbath charge.

Under the old *regime*, retaining and reproducing in colonial life the style to which in wealthy and aristocratic home circles they had been accustomed, the hospitalities of Government House were munificently administered by successive English families. Society at Headquarters was supposed to be quite select.* Fashionable entertainments were the order of the day. To the invited guest, the Lieutenant-Governor's invitation brought with it a very considerable amount of *prestige.* It formed one of the sharply defined, and sometimes arbitrarily drawn, lines by which society, at that time in the little capital, was discriminated and graded. There was considerable speculation, at the inauguration of the new Governor, in regard to the public courtesies which he might deem it expedient to adopt. Upon what principle could he harmonize practices, supposed to be of a thoroughly worldly nature, with convictions avowed, and course consistently pursued through many years of Christian profession? By those who best knew him, whatever temporary perplexities

* Like England in those days, we had quite a recognized aristocracy —Shores, Odells, Peters', Saunders', Baillies, Carters, &c.—"Reminiscences," in *Reporter.*

might arise, there was never a fear that he would
compromise his character and religious principles. A
little coterie there was, of fashionable community, especially anxious for the maintenance of a former
system. In one instance, when guests were at the
table, by a preconcerted plan partly in fun and slight-
ly in earnest, the question of a Government House Ball
was raised. The Governor received intimation that,
during incumbency of honourable office, in mode of
entertainment and of social demand, he would be expected to follow in the routine of his predecessors.
But with Hon. L. A. Wilmot, always on the alert, it
was not easy to carry a position, by any *coup-de-main*
attempt. A ball at Government House! They must
not be disappointed! He would at once name the
day! But the time indicated would not do at all;
there was an insuperable barrier. It would take them
into Lent; that was to be observed in *fasting*, and
not in feasting. The Church would not, 'during that
term of solemn Lenten services, sanction the splendour
and indulgence of worldly fashion, and of unhallowed
gratification. The inference was palpable; his course
was clear. There was a Church, from members of
which the movement had emanated, by which, during
the days of Lent, the forms and festivities pleaded
for were prohibited. For that imperative regulation
there was scrupulous and creditable concern and com-
pliance; but another church claimed from him the
same spirit of obedience. Upon the ground of principle rather than of expedience, and the year round

equally with the weeks of an annual fast, the same prohibition was enforced. In imitation of consistency, which challenged admiration and commanded fullest approval, he must decline the proposed arrangement. Promenade and musical gatherings, garden parties and *conversazione*, constituted a satisfactory and pleasant substitute. The opinion has frequently been expressed that there had never been a more generous and attractive exercise, or exhibition of Government House hospitalities.*

Until the Act of Federation, mainly representative of Imperial interests, the Lieutenant-Governors of the several Provinces were appointed immediately by the Crown. They were ordinarily selected from influential circles, aristocratic families, and the ranks of those who had claim to stations of honor and emolument. The newly-appointed Governor, under another dispensation, sustained an altered relation. In official administration, however, and in social life, he was brought into direct contact with the previous occupants of the same dignified office. But from that comparison the Hon. L. A. Wilmot could not suffer. He had that genuine dignity which springs from the soul; in all qualities, mental and physical, he was one

* Amongst prominent guests entertained by Governor and Mrs. Wilmot, during occupancy of the official mansion, were H. R. H. Prince Arthur of England, Baron and Lady Lisgar, Earl and Countess Dufferin, General Sir Hastings Doyle, Admirals Wellesley and Fanshawe, Governors Howland and Robinson. A valuable ring presented by the Prince to Mrs. Wilmot, set with diamond and emeralds, forms a fitting *souvenir* of his visit.

of nature's noblemen. There is, unquestionably, an
aristocracy of birth ; and all honor to those whose
glittering coronets have gained brighter lustre from
deeds of chivalrous worth. There is an aristocracy,
too, of wealth, in which the titles of money-kings, that
rule the world, are emblazoned and enrolled. But
there is also, higher than all, an aristocracy of mental
and moral worth, with its brilliant galaxy of names—
of which heraldry may have no record—the most
superb minds and splendid intellects that God has
ever given to the world. To the ranks of men, enobled
by worth and true magnificence of soul, by right
divine, the first native Governor of New Brunswick
belonged. " 'Tis only noble to be good."

> "He's the Noble who advances
> Freedom and the cause of man."

The duties of a Lieutenant-Governor, under ordinary
circumstances, in the Provinces of Canada, are not ex-
traordinarily onerous ; and, with moderate and average
prudence and ability, may be creditably and satisfactorily discharged. It was a matter of doubt, for many
years a popular leader, suspected of political sympathies, and quite as strongly of corresponding antipa-
thies, whether Governor Wilmot would be able to
divest himself of personal and party bias and preference. But it was soon apparent, with guarantee of
fairness to all political parties, that ample experience
of public life, and perfect acquaintance with principles
of constitutional administration, enabled him to exer-

cise a legitimate and commanding influence. Then, in
addition to the paraphernalia of governmental office,
there were many important interests which, from the
vantage ground of elevated position, he could most
effectually promote. A college commencement or the
opening of an industrial exhibition, civic ceremonial
or railway celebration, afforded opportunity that was
thoroughly utilized. Throughout the Province, every
nook of which was familiar ground, there was assured
welcome. He was intensely patriotic. As was said of
another statesman, " he loved his country as a Roman
the City of the Seven Hills ; as an Athenian the City
of the Violet Crown."

A patriotic song, " Our Dominion for ever," was
composed while at Government House. Accompanied
by music for " March or the Bivouac," it was " re-
spectfully dedicated to the Militia Forces of the Dominion, by Lieutenant-Colonel Wilmot." Two or
three stanzas may fitly close this chapter :—

> " Our Dominion for ever ! our own dear land,
>   The land of the brave and the free ;
> Wherever we roam, we'll think of our home,
>   And love the Old Banner,
>   The Red-cross Banner,
> Triumphant by land and by sea.
>
> Our Dominion for ever ! God bless our land !
>   Rose, thistle and shamrock here grow ;
> So closely entwined, they are ever combined
>   To adorn the Old Banner,
>   The Red-cross Banner,
> That triumphs o'er every foe.

E

CHORUS—Then sing our Dominion for ever !
The Queen and the Banner for ever !
No cravens are we,
By land or by sea,
We'll sing our Dominion for ever !

IV.

CHRISTIAN LIFE AND WORK.

" The power which religion should exercise over the life and conduct, is not simply like a dash of color, here and there upon the canvas ; but it is as if the canvas were dipped bodily into the color, till every thread of the fabric became saturated with it."—*Dr. Dewart's* " *Living Epistles.*"

THE facts and incidents of Hon. L. A. Wilmot's Christian life and work are closely associated with the place in which he so long resided. The city of Fredericton has many attractions. Those " who have reached it at the close of a summer's day, spent among the beautiful and ever-varying scenery of the St. John, and have glanced for a moment at the river which glides along the front of the town, at the hills which rise with gradual ascent from the rear, and at the Nashwaak which, on the opposite side, rolls its tribute of waters into the St. John, will be ready to admit that few finer situations can be found than that chosen for the capital of New Brunswick."*

* Rev. T. Watson Smith's *History of Methodism.*

During the earlier years of its history, in Fredericton, Methodism had to struggle for existence. The
steadfast Scotchman, Duncan Blair, and the little
band of which he was the leader, had to contend
with many discouragements. Probably the first strong
impetus dates from the ministry of Rev. William
Burt. The Rev. John Bass Strong, who was stationed .
there in 1827, and Revs. Richard Williams and Samp-
son Busby were all ministers of a stamp to consolidate
and extend the work. In the year 1833, after two
years upon the Mirimichi Mission, the Rev. Enoch,
now Dr. Wood, of Toronto, was appointed to the
pastorate of the Fredericton Methodist Church. A
special and distinguished style of pulpit oratory
—sound and solid exegesis, in combination with
forcible, practical appeal, sustained through all vari-
ations of tenderness, pathos, and incidental allusion
—was then in its dewy and palmy freshness and
power. It produced deep impression upon the audience,
carried the reputation of the preacher through the
community, and was blessedly and abidingly fruitful
in spiritual results. Amongst those attracted and
impressed, then at the commencement of professional
career, was the brilliant barrister, L. A. Wilmot.
Merely intellectual interest, however, soon gave place
to earnest inquiry and to profound spiritual emotion.

There was said to be at this time a settled seriousness of expression that was quite unusual to subsequent buoyancy of spirit. This may have been due
to a severe stroke of bereavement. In the early part

of 1832, Mr. Wilmot had married Jane the eldest
daughter of James Balloch, Esq., of St. John. It
was soon apparent that hectic cheek and bright eye
" were lit with the bale-fire of decline." " After a
severe and protracted illness," of some months, according to an obituary notice, "which she bore with the
greatest patience and Christian fortitude, in the full
assurance of peace with God, this amiable sufferer
breathed her last." The sweetness and sufficiency of
experimental trust in Christ, and of consolation
abundantly afforded to the sinking and suffering one,
were well calculated to produce a deep and permanent
impression upon a sensitive and affectionate nature.

Observing more than ordinary religious concern and
movement amongst the people, Mr. Wood gave notice
that, at a particular hour in the vestry, he would meet
with any who were desirous of fleeing " from the
wrath to come." The announcement was accompanied
by the emphatic explanation that, in attempting to
organize a week-night class, members of the church
were not expected to be present. He would welcome
persons who, after delay and indecision, were now determined to work out their salvation. The service
thus arranged soon came to constitute a new centre of
religious interest. Around it gathered a number of
young people, of whom the community speedily began
to take knowledge that they had been with Jesus, who
formed a valuable accession to the membership of the
church. To the minister, also, it became " a means of
grace greatly enjoyed and very highly valued ;" and

which, after nearly half a century, has still fresh and
fragrant memories.   On the first night only three persons were present, but one of these was Lemuel Allan
Wilmot.*   Solicitude for spiritual things, like the
morning dew and mist upon the mountain brow, as
ultimately proved, was not a mere transient or evanes-
cent feeling.   It deepened and developed into a
moulding influence of life.   The earnest and evangelical pastor and preacher became a valued and
trusted friend.   Through prudent counsel and salutary
influence, he was enabled to believe in Christ and to
realize conscious and satisfying rest of soul.   He
could now say, "Return unto thy rest, O my soul;
for the Lord hath dealt bountifully with thee.   For
Thou hast delivered my soul from death, mine eyes
from tears, and my feet from falling."

In the latter part of 1834, Mr. Wilmot was united
in matrimony to Miss Elizabeth Black of Halifax.
In every respect, and especially in regard to the
development of a settled religious character and stead-
fastness, the step was a most providential one.   But
sense of delicacy prevents more than a passing allusion
to one who is still with us—pursuing the even tenor
of an unobtrusive Christian course—always best
pleased, in other days, "To hear reflected from her
husband's praise her own."

An incident of social life, involving fidelity to reli-

* The other names demand record.   They were Henry Fisher, Esq.,
afterwards the efficient Superintendent of Education, and Mrs. P.
Risteen.

gious obligation, of vital importance in its bearing upon subsequent decision and consistency of Christian life, upon the authority of Dr. Wood, may be mentioned in this connection. The Watch-night service, on New Year's Eve, was at that time an impressive solemnity and largely attended. They "did not then make a sham of the watch-night." The exercises commenced at nine o'clock in the evening. "There was plenty of time for singing, praying, reading the scriptures, exhorting and preaching." It was customary on that evening for a ball, one of the great events of the year, to be given at Government House. In very different style from that of solemn and prayerful review and resolve, on the eve of 1835, they were summoned to

"Ring out the Old, ring in the New."

Young as he was, at that time, Mr. Wilmot held the military appointment of Judge Advocate. Independent of social position, an invitation was received from Sir Archibald Campbell. The testing time had come. A life-battle for Christian principle must be fought. From the days of the Hebrew Prince there have been like scenes of conflict. "What will ye see in the Shulamite? As it were the company of two armies." It was late before Mr. Wood was informed of the actual facts and the peril to which he was exposed. An affectionate message, of warning and solicitude, was immediately sent. The event was left in the hand of God. "From docility of spirit, and decisiveness previously exhibited, there was believing hope that he would re-

nounce the world, take up the cross and cling to
Christ and the Church.*   But there was also a tremulous solicitude and anxiety as to the choice and issue
of that ordeal."   In deference to official duty the first
decision was to accept the invitation.   The hour had
arrived, a coach was at the door. "Mr. Wilmot," whis-
pered a faithful friend, one who in that early day had
borne reproach· for Christ, "if Christian principle be
worth anything, it is worth everything!"   The word
was in season.   There was instantly a new and nobler
resolve.

At the commencement of the service the congregation was large.   But as the preacher's eye glanced
down the aisle and through the audience, there was
no immediate relief.   To his great gladness, however,
after the opening prayer, in fine commanding person,
followed by his youthful bride, Mr. W. was seen
making his way up to the minister's pew.   It is not
without warrant that Dr. Wood should "look upon
his decision, on that occasion, as involving the character of all the future."

The question of Church membership, though delayed for a time, had to be decisively determined.
To the Methodist Church, in the years between. have
been gathered a number of prominent and influential
laymen, that would have been a valuable accession
to any religious community.   Probably no section
of the Christian Church, in the Lower Provinces, has

---

* Mr. Wilmot was not yet in membership with the Church.

been more signally honoured. But at the time to which we now refer, nearly half a century ago, the loyalist and ecclesiastical spirit was still dominant and exclusive in New Brunswick. Cost was counted. Undeterred by any thing in the form of social ban, though no one at the time could have anticipated the complete revolution which almost immediately followed, L. A. Wilmot made his choice. He was baptized at the Communion of the Church. There was then the unalterable resolve:

> "Here in Thy courts I leave my vows,
> Let Thy rich grace record;
> Witness ye saints, that hear me now,
> If I forsake the Lord."

Though not of Methodist ancestry or antecedents, yet through Mrs. Wilmot, daughter of the Hon. William Black, grand-daughter of Rev. William Black, the apostle of Wesleyan evangelism in the Eastern Provinces, he might claim tribal inheritance in our denominational Israel. As expressive of unswerving fidelity and of affectionate allegiance in a sacred relationship, fraught only with beneficent influences, the exquisite words of Ruth the Moabitess to her Israelitish mother-in-law, found fitting application: "Entreat me not to leave thee, or to return from following after thee; for whither thou goest I will go; and where thou lodgest I will lodge; thy people shall be my people, and thy God my God; where thou diest I will die, and there will I be buried; the Lord do so

E*

to me, and more also, if aught but death part thee and
me."

There has occasionally, as apparently in the case of
Lord Macaulay—if the impression produced by Trev-
ellyan's Memoir may be trusted—in the caste and constitution of exceptionally great minds, an almost inexplicable disparity betwixt grandeur of intellect and
capacity for spiritual things, and for a life of faith
upon the Son of God. But this young lawyer, was
not more graced with gifts than gifted with grace.
Mental ability of a high order was accompanied by a
still richer endowment of moral and spiritual qualities.

Consciousness of his acceptance with God was ever
a clearly attested and experimental fact. "Through
the whole course of my religious experience," he was
known to testify, " I never once had a doubt in regard
to the question of personal salvation. The assurance
of my acceptance as a child of God, and the firmness
of my confidence, are such that Satan cannot take any
advantage on that side ; and cannot even tempt me to
doubt or fear in regard to the reality of my conversion."
A passage from Sir Humphry Davy, copied at that
time on the blank page of a book, and often referred
to in after life, expressed the ideal of coveted peace :
" I envy not any quality of mind or intellect in others ;
nor genius, power, wit, or fancy ; but if I could choose
that most delightful, and most useful to me, I should
prefer *firm religious faith* to every other blessing. It
makes life a discipline of goodness ; creates new hopes
when old hopes vanish ; throws over decay the des-

truction of existence the most gorgeous of all lights; awakens life even in death, and, from corruption and decay, calls up beauty and divinity; makes an instrument of torture and of shame the ladder of ascent to paradise; and, far above all combinations of earthly hope, calls up the most delightful visions, and plains, and amaranths; the gardens of the blest, and the security of everlasting joys, where the sensualist and the sceptic view only gloom, decay, annihilation, and despair."

Through years of unfaltering decision and service for Christ, acknowledged religious consistency combined with brilliant professional distinction, assiduous attendance upon appointed means of grace and appreciation of Christian fellowship, marked and manifest faith and fervor of spiritual faith and of spiritual and devotional exercise, in a measure and manner which compelled the homage of even thoughtless men, the genuineness of Christian character was abundantly exhibited. It was often apparent, even amidst the whirl and tumult of public life and political strife, that he had found the secret places of the Most High. It was a privilege of no common order, in that simple eloquence, almost childlike humility, and tremulous earnestness and fervor of tone, to hear him publicly plead with God.

In this case duty was supreme delight. When his eloquence was in the zenith of its splendour, and thronged audiences hung upon his lips and greeted his utterances with wild tumult of applause, as if uncon-

scious of the possession of any qualities that lifted
him above the level of the lowliest member, he devoutly and unostentatiously took his place in the
quiet and refreshing Sanctuary Service.   To him it
was no mere matter of form.   With the utmost simplicity of speech, tearful confession and tenderness of
feeling, he would bear testimony, lead in hymns of
praise, bend in sacred supplication.   Who, that has
ever been present on such an occasion, but retains
vivid impression of those fervent utterances.   They
were the distinct avowal of deep love to Christ, passionate longing for nearer intimacy with the living
Saviour, an expression of conscious dependence upon
a strong arm for help.   There was the power of pleading, prevalent petition, or the rapt fervor of silent
communion with God:

> "Sighs now breathed
> Unutterable, which the spirit of prayer
> Inspired and winged for heaven with speedier flight
> Than loudest oratory."

" During my Fredericton pastorate," says Rev. D. D.
Currie, "it was the custom to conclude the monthly
Communion Service with prayer by Judge Wilmot.
His prayers always breathed a spirit of tenderness and
devotion, and indicated his appreciation of the necessity and value of the atonement, and also how closely
he walked with God.   And many a time, in earlier
years, after he had been warring with bitter antagonists, and had been violently abused by a portion of
the press, we have heard him, in the week-night

prayer-meeting, pleading for strength and for charity, that he might stand firmly in the evil day."

The interest thus manifested, always apparent, was never more intense and demonstrative than in connection with scenes and services of revival power and blessing. To these exercises, of a special character, his emotional nature rendered him peculiarly and profoundly susceptible. In pentecostal manifestation, power from on high, and the baptism of fire, he believed and exulted. There was probably no satisfaction in life more deep and exquisite than that of witnessing evidences of penitence and exhibitions of saving mercy. Never, in brilliant efforts of public and professional life, has he seemed greater than when bowing in prayer with sorrowing suppliants; and, with affectionate eloquence, directing tearful penitents to the cross and Saviour.

The devotional element, thus conspicuously manifested, was not the only distinctive feature of Judge Wilmot's religious life. Intensity, always apparent, was not more extraordinary than the breadth and manysidedness of character. There have been others endowed with a large measure of intellectual receptiveness, of emotional feeling, of profound reverence for the Word of God, and of capacity for unwearied and life-long activities. In proportion as any of these gifts or graces have predominated, they have challenged due recognition; but in this case, in a rare degree of completeness, there was *combination* of Christian excellencies. Analogous to nature, in which he so much delighted, which finds expansion and expression in a thousand varied forms of beauty, was the outgrowth and manifestation of spiritual life. Every part and pulsation of being were pervaded and permeated by an experimental vitality that rooted itself in Christ; and, in the best forms of Christian fruitfulness, it found abundant exhibition.

It may generally be felt, in the outworking of influential lives, that all distinguishing excellencies can be traced to the operation of one simple, but potent, principle. A letter from Governor Wilmot—bearing for crest-mark, with suitable device, the significant motto : FIDE ET AMORE—dated from Government House, on the last day of 1869, contains a passage which sufficiently accounts for ceaseless, steadfast service; and which, over his whole life, throws the luminous light of heavenly law. "I feel ashamed of myself," he writes, in regard to special effort, "and am almost resolved to decline all such work for the future. But when I think how little I have done for my Saviour, and how much—*O, how much*—He has done for me, I am encouraged to go on."

Unconsciously, when called upon at a representative meeting to give the *keynote*, he indicated the dominant principle of his own life, and that which gave caste and complexion to his general religious experience and character : It was *love*—the love of God and of humanity for the love of God. "We are all one," he said; "in that we belong to the Church of Christ; and the government, essence, spirit of that Church, is love—infinite love—for as we dwell in God, we dwell in love. May that be our dwelling-place for evermore ! Amid the oppositions and trials incident to a Christian life, never let us forget that *our love must be seen.* Scarcely had the gloom settled down upon the Garden of Gethsemane, than that matchless love was poured down upon men. It has passed down through the ages, and is the woof and warp of religious experience."

The infinite, inexhaustible, everlasting love of God in Christ, inexplicable in its manifestations,—until the harmonies and ascriptions of earth and heaven blend and burn into one mighty magnificent chorus—never to be adequately celebrated, was a subject on which he delighted to dwell. It fired his soul and filled his mental vision. "The love of God," he wrote in a valued communication, "is a vast abyss, an immeasurable expanse. Along its shores, from age to age, with lengthened and added weight, the plummet of angel-mind has sought to sound the mystery. But the cry has ever been : ' *O, the depth!* ' "

> " In vain the first-born seraph tries
> To sound the depth of love Divine."

In conviction of the compassionate and unerring love of God, his own heart found firm and secure refuge ; and, from the same inexhaustible source, he was often enabled to communicate consolation. In answer to a note, informing him of a sore bereavement, he wrote : " Fresh wounds deep in the heart, and old wounds opened! Your heart-sorrow I cannot inter-meddle with. But most certainly the rod was in the hand of Infinite Love. The purpose may be hidden now, but you will know it by-and-by; and your sorrow hereafter, will be followed by a higher note of praise. '*All things work together for good.*' Work together—that is *harmonize.* Wondrous harmony! It is harmony made up of deepest heart-sorrow and abounding joy—pain and suffering of body and peace of soul—deepest abasement of spirit and joy unspeakable and full of glory—self-condemnation and faith, justification—having nothing and yet possessing all things. What a marvellous combination and variety of tones, and yet a heavenly harmony! May you find consolation in the conscious assurance of this harmony of love! And while you attentively listen, may you find it becoming sweeter and deeper until the wearied heart shall breathe forth in unison its own assurance, *He doeth all things well.*"

No one can have come into close contact with Judge Wilmot without being struck with his profound veneration for the Word of God. *The law of God was in his heart.**

A copy of the Scriptures long used bears evident attestation of the manner in which he was accustomed to

---

* "In one of my visits to the House of Assembly, during the days of stormy debate, there was a most memorable scene, Mr. Wilmot held the Bible in his hand. To that standard of immutable law, and of authoritative enactment, he made Supreme appeal."— *Rev. J. Sutcliffe.*

study the sacred page. He meditated therein by day and night. There are *marks* to indicate successive readings of the Bible—teachings through which he had been led to nearer communion with God—familiar passages which in a memorable moment had become luminous with heavenly light—practical truths which had been as a light to his feet and a lamp to his path and in the keeping of which there had been great reward—inspired words that had been interwoven with the eventful incidents of his history—messages breathing the spirit of infinite tenderness and richly fraught with consolation—precepts unto which in his way he had taken heed, and by which his life had been purified—radiant promises which in the dark and murky night had suddenly gleamed out as stars of hope—the twenty-third psalm in which many an experience of life found its most fitting expression— the ninety-first psalm which before starting upon a journey he was accustomed to read at the family altar. Through and through, the Book of Psalms specially bears evidence of habitual and prayerful perusal. In its simple and pathetic energy there was an irresistible charm. "Think," he said, "of such passages as—'*I cried unto the Lord,*' and, '*Out of the depths have I cried unto Thee, O Lord!*' One can scarcely repeat that word '*cry*' without a sigh or tear. It sounds like the sob of childhood and suits the tender spirit." There was also keen appreciation of the poetic beauty and grand imagery of the Hebrew Bard. The woof of experimental testimony in the

fervor of Christian fellowship, was shot with many
a thread of inspired utterance : " I will abide in Thy
tabernacle for ever : I will trust in the covert of Thy
wings.   For Thou, O God, hast given me the heritage
of those that fear Thy name."   From the New Testament, in the same way, there were passages that
glowed with celestial fire : " Whom having not seen ye
love ; in whom though now ye see Him not, yet believing, ye rejoice with joy unspeakable and full of
glory."

With acute and devout interest, he followed up the
main points at issue between the Bible and extreme ex-
ponents of modern science.   Many of the best authorities upon these subjects were constantly at hand for
repeated perusal.   A volume from his library now before me, of considerable value as an exact and exhaustive discussion, in margin and underline, bears evidence of painstaking investigation and of clear mastery
of complex and controverted questions.   In one of his
later public addresses, at a meeting held in Erskine
Church, Montreal, the audience including a number of
young men, he expatiated upon this theme :

" Some scientists and leading thinkers, as Darwin,
Huxley, and Tyndall, whose marvellous and dangerous
essays denied the power of prayer, and sought to prove
to mankind that they were mere evolutions or a
development from a lower sphere of life.   There was a
danger here. He also referred to a materialistic system
of infidelity, wherein the author blasphemously introduced into his creed a Trinity, composed of humanity,

earth, and heaven. Was this his God? Could he pray to the sky above him, the earth beneath him, or to humanity? What could poor humanity do, even in its most elevated, learned form to aid him? Young men would have to rigidly guard themselves against these revolting forms of infidelity. In this connection, it afforded the speaker much pleasure to see the able manner in which Dr. Dawson had dissected the Darwinian theory, and shown the falsity of such reasoning, by clear and unanswerable argument. They could rest assured that wherever science contradicted the Bible, it would be proved to be in the wrong; that wherever a scientific statement has been discovered to be perfectly true, it always coincided with the Biblical record. There was a remarkable illustration of this in the deciphering of a number of cuneiform inscriptions in the East, where, in every instance in which they illustrated Old Testament history, there was not found the first contradiction. The recorders of the Old Testament history were proved and not found wanting in truth and accuracy; they were honest, and called a spade a spade. They wrote their own nation's history with the same impartiality and candour with which they penned that of others. They covered up no one's sins and shortcomings, not even those of their own brethren; and he loved the Book the more he pondered on the honest, straightforward dealing of those writers of old." *

* *Witness.*

A few years ago, Fredericton was a garrison city.
Military gentlemèn and their families constituted an
important and influential element of social life.   The
Government of the Province was, for a time, administered by the General in command of the troops.   At a
dinner party, largely attended, some question of religious or Biblical character was incidentally mooted. An
officer of high position in the army, and of considerable dash and celerity in conversation, frankly avowed
his scepticism.   The accuracy of sacred historic fact
was impugned.   In the sweep of scientific discovery,
and the march of modern thought, like the Talmud,
the Vedas, and the Koran, it would be left behind.   It
belonged to a former age, and was merely one of the
many land-marks of human progress. Judge Wilmot's
veneration for the inspired volume was well known ;
bound up with that book divine were the noblest
hopes of his life.   It was not a moment, and he was
not in a mood, for silence.   Recently he had read,
almost devoured, the " Old Red Sandstone," and other
works of Hugh Miller.   In reference to the question,
raised for disputation, he was thoroughly informed ;
and, in force and felicity of expression, there were few
who could meet him on equal terms.   The gauntlet
fearlessly thrown down was promptly accepted.   Like
chaff from an Oriental threshing floor, the objections
were speedily scattered to the wind.   The claims of
God's word were triumphantly vindicated.   Never did
his countenance light up with a finer glow than when
avowing attachment to the book of revealed truth :—

"Should all the forms that men devise
    Assault my faith with treacherous art,
I'll call them vanity and lies,
    And bind thy Gospel to my heart."

In Judge Wilmot, as an ordinary hearer, the preacher in fulfilment of his mission and message, found uniformly an appreciative and responsive spirit. The ministry of the Gospel was regarded by him as the divinely appointed and approved agency and instrumentality for the world's regeneration; and ministers of Christ, charged with onerous duty, were esteemed for their work's sake. If the occasion demanded, and, instead of earnest, faithful, and affectionate exposition and application, there had been an apparent attempt at display—what he would have characterized as pulpit rocket-shooting—he could subject the efforts to searching criticism. But the prevailing habit of attention was that of devout, lowly, sympathetic feeling, and withal a striving to profit. With the minister, his intercourse was that of a frank, genial, helpful, and brotherly spirit. Some of us can remember days of weakness, and comparatively inexperienced effort, when the thought of the Judge's presence, and the ordeal of his searching criticism, produced a good deal of tremor and occasionally embarrassment; but a glance from his kindly eye and interested expression brought relief. A word of heart-uttered kindness, at the close, has nerved the timid, shrinking messenger to renewed courage and resolve. "In the beginning of my ministerial career, when for the first time ap-

pointed to preach on a Sabbath morning in the Fredericton Church, waiting tremblingly in the preacher's
vestry for the appointed moment to arrive, Judge
Wilmot favoured me with a call. We had not seen
each other for a year, and now, knowing my timidity
as a youthful public speaker, he had come in advance
of the service to give me a cordial welcome. He laid
his hand on my shoulder, and spoke a few kind and
encouraging words, which greatly strengthened me for
the duties of that occasion. He was one of the best
hearers any pastor ever had." *

In conscientious and habitual attendance at the
week-night and social services of the church, always
to him a source of strength and time of refreshing
from the presence of the Lord, the Hon. L. A. Wilmot
presented an example worthy of imitation. "In his
attendance to all the ordinances of the Church," according to the testimony of Dr. Wood, going back to
earliest membership, "he was regular, interrupted
only by occasional public duties; for, very early after
completing his professional duties, he entered the
tumultous arena of politics—forced out by the irresistible voice of the electors of York County." During
the most active years of his life, when as a point of
expediency it might not have been deemed politic to
forego legitimate social advantage, with successive
Lieutenant-Governors, some of whom were not quite
able to comprehend the necessity for that amount of
religious strictness, for himself and Mrs. Wilmot, like-

* Rev. D. D. Currie.

minded in this essential matter, upon regular week-
night services of the church, there was an understanding that invitations to official dinners and other social
arrangements must be declined. To the Methodist
Church in Fredericton, when I first went to reside
there, I found him to be a pillar of strength. I
can still seem to see him, so vivid are the recollections
of that time, as he took his accustomed place in the
prayer-meeting. Flanked by several official brethren,
then a noble band, he always occupied the same seat
to the right of the desk. With an unrivalled voice,
and often a full heart, he was ever ready to sing,
or speak, or pray. Often some passing incident, or an
utterance of the occasion, was turned to good account.
"I am just holding on," some one remarked. The
suggestiveness of the phrase was brought out. We
could see a tempest-tossed bark "holding on" in the
troubled waters of some dangerous roadstead, or off a
wild lea-shore. The waves beat high ; but the anchor
was sure. As voyagers to eternity, we had often
to breast the wave. We had to *hold on*. The angry
tempest would speedily subside. The freighted bark
of life would yet—

> "Sail o'er sunnier seas"
> Than claspt of old the Hesperides ;
> A bark whose sails by angel hands,
> Are furled on a strand of golden sands."

In regard to Christian *fellowship*, "the communion
of saints," for which in the Methodist Church special
provision is made, Judge Wilmot formed the highest

estimate. He was accustomed to speak of this means
of grace as the *sheet anchor* of his earlier religious life.
During the pastorate of Rev. I. Sutcliffe, in 1844, he
was appointed to the responsible office of leader.
Around him, from time to time, were gathered many
gifted young men, now widely scattered, several of
them in the ministry of the Church to whom that
service was a moulding influence. From that class
they graduated as efficient and successful workers for
Christ. A paragraph, supposed to be from the pen of
an accomplished minister of the Methodist Episcopal
Church,* indicates the cherished recollections which
still cling to that scene of hallowed intercourse : " His
class for many years had been the school for spirit-
uality and instruction. Warm and tender in sympathy, humble and simple among his brethren, faithful
in admonition, inspiring in address, and powerful in
example, many will count it as among their richest
privileges to have been associated with him. Often
have young men gone discouraged from the world
and ready to give up ; but his words have gathered
up all their scattered resolutions, given new warmth
to their zeal, courage to their hearts, strength to their
purpose, and on retiring there has been the determination : '*Nothing, nothing shall separate me from the
love of God.*' Under the administration of such a
leader, the service could never degenerate into dull,
insipid routine. It was hallowed by fervent prayer,

---

*Rev. T. Berton Smith. Revs. George S. Milligan and D. D. Currie
were members of that class.

brightened by sacred song, enlivened by experience
and testimony, and energised by apt application of
apposite passages from the familiar pages of God's
Word. Often 'one mightier than the leader was
there.'"

> " Heaven's gate
> Is opened by their psalm. Then do they state
> Their glad experience, or anxious :
> What meed of blessing, or what bounteous share
> Of Mercy's richest gifts, has been this freight.
> Ah ! as they speak their lifted hearts catch fire ;
> Their souls are flames, their thoughts are ecstasies,
> And heaven's own glory on their face is laid.
> Such earnest hours makes men's resolves the higher ;
> Such fervent men fulfil high purposes :
> And humble men, e'en thus, are nobles made.

It is of essential interest and importance, for the
glory of God, the honour of the Redeemer, the welfare
of the Church, and the triumph of Christianity, that
the spirit of devotion and consecration should find expression in appointed religious services. But it is also
requisite, for the same imperative reason, especially
on the part of Christian men and women, that a living
present principle of religion and testimony for Christ
should be carried into every sphere and domain of
life.

The consistency of Hon. L. A. Wilmot, maintained
through many years, constituted a genuine mark of
the validity and sterling worth of profession and Christian character. There was no tendency to compromise; his colors were at the top of the mast. In open

F

fold, they proclaimed fearless adhesion to principle.
By unshrinking avowal of conviction, practical obedience to sacred injunction, unswerving loyalty to the
Saviour, his attitude and influence were felt and
acknowledged. For the amalgamation of Church and
world, fashion and religion, there was never any
insidious attempt. "Would you say of any one place
of fashionable gaiety," asks Dr. Chalmers, "that it
makes a good ante-chamber of preparation for that
house of solemn interview in which converse is held,
either with the still, small voice within, or with that
God above who bids you sanctify Him at all times in
your hearts, and to do all things to His glory?" There
are scenes and circles, bringing with them the taint of
worldliness, the very atmosphere of which is absolutely unfriendly to communion with God, into which
some professedly Christian people thoughtlessly and
foolishly plunge, that he habitually and cautiously
avoided.

"As I grow older, my views are changing fast as to
the degree of conformity to the world which we
should allow. The door at which those influences
enter, which countervail parental instruction and
example, I am persuaded is, *yielding to the ways of
good society.* By dress, books, and amusements, an
atmosphere is formed which is not that of Christianity. More than ever do I feel that we must stand
in a kind but determined opposition to the fashions
of the world, breasting the waves like the Eddystone
lighthouse. And I have found nothing yet which

requires more courage and independence than to rise
a little, but decidedly above, the *par* of the religious
world around us.   Sure, the way in which we commonly go on is not the self-denial and sacrifice and
cross-bearing which the New Testament talks of.
' Then is the offence of the cross ceased.'   Our slender
influence on the circle of our friends is often to be
traced to our leaving so little difference between us
and them." *

As the leader of a great political party, Mr. Wilmot
could not always avoid personal difficulty.   The ordeal
came in due time ; and, for his religious character,
constituted a crucial test.   To some such incident of
party conflict, in 1844, he has been known to refer
with much feeling.   There had been an attempt, by
means of defamation and slanderous assertion, to
weaken his great and growing influence in the country.
There was no bar-sinister on his escutcheon.   But
he had the pride of birth, of pure, unsullied name and
of high, incorruptible integrity, which such a man can
feel.   There was the proud sensitiveness of a noble
nature and a chivalrous contempt for coarse, personal
invective.   With all militant qualities he was abundantly endowed.   But for the restraint of Christian
principle and the dictates of supreme law, for insult
and injury, the first impetuous prompting of passion
might have been to demand the satisfaction which a
now happily obsolete code of honour prescribed.   In
such a mood and moment came the wonted hour of

* Dr. J. W. Alexander, of Princeton.

family worship, that ordinarily brought with it an atmosphere of peace, pure feeling and of tranquil
thought. A juncture had been reached in which there
was need, if ever, to take heed in the way according
to God's word and to ponder that pure commandment
which enlightened the eyes. Irritated and exasperated,
with a deep thunder-frown upon his brow, but still
battling bravely with his own spirit, for the moment
he turned away from the Book and the altar of devotion. But there was by his side one gifted with qualities of mind and temper, most needed as the comple-
ment of his own, who comprehended the magnitude of
the crisis. It was of the utmost consequence, before
plunging afresh into the excitement of debate and
possibly of renewed aggravation, that conscience and
calm judgment should assert their supremacy. With
the Bible, he was followed from the room ; and, by the
highest and most sacred of all considerations, was en-
treated to seek counsel where it had never failed.
Yielding to the pressure, which could not well be re-
sisted, the Book was opened, and, incidentally, his eye
rested upon a passage in Job. Four thousand years ago
the Patriarch of Uz had passed through a like ordeal ;
and the ancient, unchangeable promise was still as a
direct message from God :—" And thine eye shall be
clearer than the noonday ; thou shalt shine forth, thou
shalt be as the morning ; yea thou shalt dig about thee
and thou shalt take thy rest in safety. Also thou shalt
lie down and none shall make thee afraid ; yea many
shall make their suit unto thee."

The victory was complete. From the land of Uz, for his comfort, the message of God had been sounding along the corridors of ages. Suggestions of inspired record wove themselves into petition, and help for the hour of need was earnestly and humbly implored. He was refreshed by conscious communion with God. From the discipline of sore trial came self-conquest. In force and firmness of resolve, he was strengthened for the exigency that was pressing hard upon him; and, as the result, was enabled to exercise that noble spirit of forgiveness which Christianity inculcates. "Every part of that passage," said Judge Wilmot in after years, "has had a literal accomplishment." In Government House, which at that time he occupied, after retirement of other guests and members of his own family, a frequent and favoured occurrence of such visits, he indulged in reminiscences of that period of life. With evident satisfaction he recounted incidents of that memorable episode in his history. Each part of the promise, as in the life of the Arabian Patriarch, had received a minute and marvellous fulfilment. His age had been clearer than the noonday. The sun of life, then in evening declination, was sinking to the horizon in a clear and serene sky. He had dug about him; and beneath the ample shade and rich foliage of trees, planted by his own hand, now found quiet and peaceful repose. Many, including children of those who sought petty party advantage, had made their suit unto him.

"I had heard much of Mr. Wilmot," said a gentle-

man of the civil service. "Political asperities were
then at their height. Insensibly my feeling towards
him had yielded to prejudice. The first time we met
was in a social service of the Church. There was
a slight allusion to some unmerited aspersion and
to the value of an untarnished Christian character.
But if they only knew, he said, in tender and
tremulous tone, what I know myself of weakness, failure, imperfection, they might say worse
things than now. The genuineness of feeling and
of a noble spirit, that could only stand abashed in
the presence of an infinite purity, were not to be
mistaken."

The laureate, Mr. Tennyson, claims for his Red-
Cross Knight* that on him "the loyal-hearted hung;"
that "the serpent at his side" ceased "to flicker with
its double-tongue," and that—

> "His strength was as the strength of ten
> Because his heart was pure."

In refreshing relief to the strain and tension of
continued contest, and the asperities inseparable from
public life, in such a period of political convulsion,
we come upon scenes of gentle and peaceful ministry :

> "He who ascends to mountain tops shall find
> Their loftiest peaks most wrapt in clouds and snow."

But, even amidst the towering summits and the everlasting snows of Mont Blanc, some of the loveliest

---

* Sir Galahad.

and most exquisite forms of vegetable life may be discovered. The Alpine traveller finds a sheltered and sunny spot, protected by frozen peaks, on which the sun's rays, reflected from glittering ice, beat down with double force, where rare and beautiful flowers and plants bloom and luxuriate.

Genuiness of Christian character, in the lives of public men, must bear scrutiny beneath a light that beats fiercely along their track. But there are many quiet and unobtrusive ways, and kind and gentle deeds in which the best qualities of heart and life find practical expression. " Pure religion in the sight of God and the Father is this, to visit the fatherless and the widow in their affliction." In the most active and influential period of life, Judge Wilmot was prompt and faithful in visitation of the sick. The lowlier members of the Church, equally with those of more prominent social position, were kept in view. Many a sufferer was refreshed by the beaming light of Christian sympathy, and strengthened by tender and loving words. The poor were remembered in his ministrations, and destitution relieved. In an appeal on their behalf, during the season of " peace and good-will," the preacher selected for his theme the words of the King : " For I was an hungered, and ye gave Me meat; I was thirsty, and ye gave Me drink ; I was a stranger, and ye took Me in ; naked, and ye clothed Me ; I was sick, and ye visited Me ; I was in prison, and ye came unto Me." The contrast was also emphasised. " I

escaped that lash," he afterwards said, "my pensioners
were first provided for."

Few members of the Methodist portion of the community can have visited the city of Fredericton, where
a beautiful and nobly-proportioned church with lofty
spire looks down upon the broad and sweeping river,
and the adjacent country for miles distant, without
something of admiration and, perhaps, a tinge of denominational pride. It is inferior only to the chaste
and costlier cathedral structure of the same city, and
to the magnificent sanctuary—a gem of architecture—at
Marysville, on the opposite side of the river.* It is now
with interest remembered, upon nearing that city almost
a quarter of a century ago, then just arrived from
England, curious in regard to all facts and phases of
colonial life, how standing out to the depths of vaulted
azure, gleaming in the light of the setting sun, the
lofty spire of that church became an object of prominent and thrilling interest.

The Fredericton Church has a record worth knowing about, and a history into which many a thread
of Judge Wilmot's time and thought and means and
life were woven. In the old Methodist *chapel*, as
then usually designated, during the decade, 1840-50,
were gathered a noble band of men and women—
as splendid a group of families as any community
could show. The Church at that time was deemed
comfortable and sufficiently capacious. In a special

---

* Erected for Methodist worship by the munificence of Alexander
Gibson, Esq.

effort comprising many munificent contributions, a heavy debt, the encumbrance of years was liquidated. Scarcely had this long and devoutly wished for consummation been accomplished when there came the sweep and desolation of a great conflagration. A large part of the city, and most of the homes and business establishments of families forming part of that congregation, were destroyed. Stunned and bewildered with their own losses, their habitations smouldering in ruins, there were many that grieved not less sorely for the *holy and beautiful house which had been burned with fire.*

The dislocation produced by such a sweeping disaster, in many of our chief centres, is well known ; and how it tests the material and the mould of men. On the part of some, discouraged by the magnitude and complication of difficulties thickening around them, there was almost an utter paralysis ; and, for Church enterprise, a fear of complete collapse. Their homes were in ashes, business places burnt, the trade of the city prostrate, their available resources greatly reduced ; and how, therefore, could they meet the emergency with any hope of success. But Judge Wilmot, whose own available means were freely pledged to the object, proposed that at once they should arise and build. "Brethren," he said, as they met in consultation, "let us start for a larger and more elegant church." He was desirous of securing a spacious edifice, in modern style of architecture, that would meet the necessities of their families, accommodate the large Sunday-

F*

school, consolidate their work ; and, as became a metropolitan structure, constitute an ornament and attraction to the city.   The overmastering impulse and
indomitable energy, with which objections and obstacles were encountered and surmounted, fully prevailed.   Trustees and others caught the contagion,
and moved with the inspiration of his courage and
hope.   From the acceptance of plans and the laying
of the foundation stone, through all stages of the work,
until the scaffolding had been removed, he watched
its progress.   "The labour of his own hand," says a
public correspondent, cognizant of all the facts and
probably a contributor to the enterprise, "on the
church edifice hastened the too tardy efforts of mechanics."

By not a few, however, that superb ecclesiastical
erection was keenly criticised.   The propriety of
magnificent enterprise, and of a noble faith that
prompted and sustained the builders, was questioned.
It was beyond the means of the worshippers.   There
was excessive ornament that involved serious expenditure ; the spire was too ambitious.   There were—

> "Storied windows richly dight
> Casting a dim, religious light."

Some of the most estimable members delighted to
recall blessed services, rich and hallowed manifestations of spiritual power, marvellous conversions, rapturous fellowship with which their earlier history had
been favored.   A plain building, without architectural

pretensions, it was thought by some, would have been more congenial to the tastes of a people nurtured without anything of material splendour in the surroundings of their worship. Until about that time, the Methodist Churches of the Province, and mostly those of other denominations, were of the same uniform and broadside pattern. The more modern style of Church architecture, while creditable to the taste of the worshipping community, may vindicate at least an equal claim to the motto of ancient ecclesiastical builders: *Soli Deo gloria*, "to God alone be the glory." Had the edifice then erected, as some desired, conformed to the old outlines of idea, it would have been at once antiquated. The golden opportunity for improvement would have passed beyond their reach. Fortunately, Judge Wilmot had caught the spirit of modern Church architecture, and prevailed in plan and purpose.

The *Choir* of the Church in Fredericton, for more than thirty years, was led by Judge Wilmot. That onerous charge was first undertaken in 1845. His heart was always in the work; in congregational worship he found abundant enjoyment. With John Milton he could say :—

> " There let the pealing organ blow,
> To the full-voiced choir below,
> In service light and anthem clear ;
> As may with sweetness, through mine ear,
> Dissolve me into eastasies
> And bring all heaven before my eyes."

"Passionately fond of music, able to perform on almost any instrument, with a quick ear and an excellent voice, a highly cultivated taste, the nicest power of adapting a tune to a hymn and an anthem to the occasion, and with great command over all performers, he has rare qualifications for this important service ; and he is not one of your fastidious choristers that can only sing in state and with the artistic. He sings everywhere, ' where two or three are gathered,' and with the children ; from the chorus richly rendered before the large congregation, he comes easily to ' I want to be an angel ' amongst the little ones of the infant class. The present generation of singers has grown up under his influence and training." *

There was generally, in the management of choir-service, an exquisite adaptation of musical expression to the theme and structure of the hymn. The Rev. Mr. Sutcliffe, whose reminiscences of that period are still fresh and vivid, mentions an illustrative incident. The organ was just then introduced, and renewed impetus given to congregational singing. An Incarnation hymn, "Plunged in a gulf of dark despair," was announced. It has one of those sudden transitions that perplex sensitive musicians. After striking a note of sadness and gloom, it rises to a strain of exulting rapture :—

"O for this love let rocks and hills
Their lasting silence break."

* *Zion's Herald*, Boston.

But, on that occasion, with surprise and fine effect, the tune was changed, and the closing stanzas rendered with a joyous burst of melody and triumph.

In the discussion of the Hymn and Tune Book question at the Toronto General Conference, there was a point of Judge Wilmot's speech which very distinctly showed his musical taste and tendency. In illustration of the power and pathos of music and song, he referred to an incident of missionary encounter with arbitrary and powerful chieftains. As an intimation that this teacher could not proceed, except at the peril of his life, their spears were crossed upon his path. Comprehending the situation, the Missionary tuned his violin and produced harmonies of sound that moved and thrilled their savage souls. Ferocity was subdued, and, melted into tenderness, they became friends to help him on his way. The special charm of the story was in pathetic and dramatic power of description. Unconsciously and in perfect pantomime, with ease and attitude and consummate grace of gesture, he went through the process—tuned the instrument, touched each vibrating chord, and drew a stroke that an amateur at once recognized as the play of an old practitioner. Then came the application of the incident, and not a few, moved at first to laughter, found a tear wetting the cheek.

Hymns of sevens and sixes, in Methodist worship, are not the rolling iambics for which there are appropriate tunes in abundance; they are in the more plaintive tone of the trochiac measure to which, for

special themes of a penitential character, Charles
Wesley seems to have given decided preference. They
usually contain, in each stanza, an eight-syllable line ;
hence there is some difficulty, in current music, in
obtaining sufficient and satisfactory variety of tunes
for that class of hymns. In this fact will be found
explanation of a passage dated at Government House.
" I have been looking up," he wrote from the confine-
ment of a sick room, " and copying out for the choir
some choice tunes for seven and six hymns. We are
rather deficient in variety ; but with this accession we
shall be ready. I think it as much *the duty of the
congregation to furnish good music,* for Sabbath worship and praise, as it is for the minister to prepare and
preach good sermons ; and, while I can look after it,
shall do what I can for that department of Church
service."

A favorite idea of Judge Wilmot, on which he loved
to linger, was that the Incarnation song of the angelic
choristers—" Glory to God in the highest "—was only
the prelude of an eternal anthem strain. Sweeping
through space, it filled the universe ; and, before the
throne of God, rolled up into magnificent chorus.*
"And if only," he would say, " the music of that

---

* " Does not Scripture bear him out ? Does it not ring with
music ? Does it not tell us how at the creation ' the morning stars
sang together and all the sons of God shouted for joy ?' And as the
Bible begins with the song of the morning stars over man created and
ends with the sevenfold chorus of hallelujahs and harping symphonies
over man redeemed, so its central moment, uniting both, is that carol
of angels at the Saviour's birth."—*Canon Farrar.*

heavenly song had been *dotted* down, we might have had some idea of seraphic melody!" At musical practice he often made reference to the song and service of heaven, and once longingly said : " O may I bear some humble part in that immortal song—if nothing more that I may be permitted to hold the music for David's harp!" "But," said one of the singers, in reference to his passionate love for training voices and leading in sacred song, that was perfectly understood, "Judge, would that satisfy you?" "Would you not like *to lead the whole choir?*" "Well, yes," he replied, with amused interest and a pleasant smile, "perhaps, I should. But I must praise Him in some way."

The members of the choir, which comprised some sweet and superb voices, were chiefly drafted from the *Sabbath-school.* We come now, so far as Christian life was concerned, to the principal scene of action. In the Fredericton Sunday-school, for many years, the Hon. L. A. Wilmot found a throne of power. There, if nowhere else, he was "the czar of many lands.' The earliest records, accessible to the Secretary,* date back only to 1833—corresponding with the period of conversion and not improbably the commencement of a Sunday-school career. On June 14th, 1835, he was appointed Assistant Superintendent. The exact date of his first appointment as *Superintendent* has not been entered, in the usual form, upon the records of the School. It is thought to have been in 1843. He

---

* Geo. A. Perley, Esq.,—who, for *twenty-eight,* years has efficiently discharged the duties of that office.

was then, probably, conscious of the grand possibilities
of his life in that direction, of the magnificence of re-
sponsibilities involved, or of the extent to which the
impress of his noble and splendid enthusiasm should
be stamped upon that institution of our Church—for
soon after the office seems to have been resigned. The
pressure of professional and political duties and en-
gagements, in that period of fierce and incessant warfare, may have interfered with thorough and satisfactory preparation for the arduous and onerous duties
of such a post. Judicial appointment would promise
ampler opportunity for Biblical research. "A great
luminary," says Mr. Fenety, in his valuable Notes,
"set in semi-darkness on the day that Mr. Wilmot
left the Forum for the Bench. He was the light
of the House for seventeen years, the centre from
whence radiated most of the sparkling gems in the
political firmament. It was at a time of life, for he
was comparatively a young man, and at a period when
talents such as his were mostly wanted by his party
and the country." But the loss of the State was
the gain of the Church. In January 1851, following
the record, he became the teacher of a large Bible-
class. On January 11th, 1853, came a distinction
which was subsequently regarded as the most honourable of his life. He was again appointed to the
Superintendency of the School; and, until the day
previous to his death,—which took place May 20th,
1878—for twenty-five years continuously, with deep-

ening and growing interest and attachment, he faithfully fulfilled the duties of that important office.

In the Sunday-school Judge Wilmot, as for so many years he was affectionately designated, found his element. He now believed in the grand possibilities of that agency with all the convictions and sympathies of his intellectual and moral being. Without stint or grudge, for the advantage of his charge, he lavished the best treasures of his opulent and original mind. The whole institution, through all its arrangements and exercises, felt the inspiration and elasticity of his presence. There was a magnetism in his movements and ceaseless activity and tone that were all but irresistible. In matters of perplexity the teachers were counselled; and, by a beaming smile, they were stimulated and encouraged. Inefficiency was rebuked by the sense and consciousness of an intense earnestness. A tardy scholar was roused to energy. Diligence was recognized and rewarded. Disobedience was awed and abashed by the severity of look or tone. There was that in his frown and word which was terror to evil doers. The stubborn and rebellious, by affectionate admonition and tenderness of appeals, always a gratifying result, were not unfrequently subdued to penitential acknowledgment. Each department, while under his cognizance, was held responsible for special work. Aided by an efficient assistant,* and a noble staff of officers and teachers, mostly of his own training, the entire operations of the School were carried on

* S. D. McPherson, Esq.

with the ease and smoothness of the most perfect and
polished mechanism.

A main attraction, for many years, was in the
addresses which from time to time formed part of
the closing exercises. The substance of many public
lectures, commanding grand audiences and enthusiastic interest, were first given at the Sunday-school.
At the time of my arrival in Fredericton, during the
winter 1855-6, the Judge was commencing a series
of such addresses which alike attracted children,
teachers and strangers. There were incidents and
episodes of Bible-history—the venerable Bede's de-
parting doxology—Wycliff's trial before Archbishop
Courtnay—the reading of a chained Bible in the
crypt of St. Paul's—the martyrdom of Lady Anne
Askew at Smithfield, and of Ridley and Latimer
at Oxford—which, as then vividly described, could
never be forgotten, and which were the means of
making many a student of the annals of the Reform-
ation. The flash of eye kindling into sympathy with
the subject and magnetic thrill of tone, as he caught
the prophetic spirit of the Reformer's undaunted
testimony—"The truth shall prevail"—even at this
distance of time stands out in living interest; and
Tyndal's memorable utterance, in reply to irritated
ecclesiastics—"If God spare my life, ere many years
I will cause a boy that driveth the plough to know
more of the Scriptures than you do"—seemed, as
it rolled past us through the centuries, to throb with
all its original force and significance. There was also

a rare fascination, for such an audience, and deeply instructive, in the allegory of John Bunyan—the immortal dreamer. It was accompanied by illustrative scenes of the Slough of Despond, the House of the Interpreter, the Palace called Beautiful, the dreadful Fight with the Foul Fiend, Doubting Castle, the Delectable Mountains, the Enchanted Ground, the Land of Beulah, and that mysterious River crossed by the Pilgrims—where, accompanied by the shining ones, and the trumpets all sounding around them, they passed up through the golden gates into the glorious city. Books of travel, marvels of science, the culture of nature, an exhaustless fund of incident, for instruction and gratification, were also placed under exacting contribution. But especially did this honoured Superintendent delight to expound the Word of God, and from the richest of all treasures to bring out things new and old. There were some selections, as for example the Ten Commandments, portions of the Sermon on the Mount, Narratives of the Evangelists, the Twelfth of Romans, and other teachings of Holy Scripture, to which repeated attention was turned ; and, because of the setting which in wealth of thought he gave, many a gem of inspired truth was seen to flash with a brighter and purer glow. Indelible has been the impression thus produced by a passage such as that in Proverbs :—" Let not mercy and truth forsake thee : bind them about thy neck ; write them on the table of thy heart : so shalt thou find favor

and good understanding in the sight of God and
man."

Is it right that there should be anything of unique
interest in the supreme consecration of splendid intellectual gifts to such a department of Christian work?
May not the very best minds and richest culture,
which churches and congregations can possibly supply,
find in the Sunday-school an ample sphere? "Virtue
and intelligence," according to Chief-Justice Marshall,
an eminent Jurist of the United States, "are the
basis of our independence and the conservative principles of national and individual happiness; and
Sunday-school institutions are devoted to the protection of both." "The common school," says Sir
Charles Reed, a member of the British Parliament,
and a devoted Sunday-school worker, "contemplates
the physical, intellectual and moral being; the Sunday-
school, the religious and spiritual. The public school
has its limits; but the Sunday-school knows none, for
its teaching crowns and glorifies the completely
educated man."

Reluctantly consenting, on a Sunday-school Anniversary occasion, to conduct the service, a passage was
very appropriately selected: *Suffer little children to
come unto me, and forbid them not; for of such is the
kingdom of God.* " I have heard him," said one of the
most intelligent of his auditors, "at the Bar, in the
Legislature, on the Bench and the platform, but never
with a more genuine satisfaction than in the service of
to-day."

Amongst recollections of influence and usefulness, fragrant as the breath of a summer morning, running along the line of many bright and happy years, bringing out the best and most benign qualities of a noble and beautiful character and sympathy, were numerous incidents which must fail to find any adequate record : exquisite renderings of tuneful melodies and of strains sweet and familiar as household words—visits to the sick room, eagerly anticipated ; winged petitions and tender, loving words, where fever or consumption was wasting the child of weakness—scenes, "privileged beyond the common walks of virtuous life, quite on the verge of heaven," where brightness suffusing the countenance of the sufferer was eloquently expressive of strength renewed and of the unutterable gratification afforded—touching and yet exulting reference to the early departure of some beloved member of his charge ; of triumph over death, life radiant with immortality, and the consummated blessedness and fulness of the beatific vision. Delineation of memories such as these, that linger with us like the thought of a beautiful vision, demands the pencil and inspiration of genius, and, in this sober sketch, may not be attempted.

In the mere fact of elevation to distinctions and dignities of public and official life, because of infirmities incident to humanity, may not unfrequently be found a searching and a severe test of the validity and genuineness of principle and Christian character. The present Lord Chancellor of England—the successor of

illustrious men and of imperial minds—one of the
most distinguished members of the Conservative
Cabinet—is a faithful and self-denying Sunday-school
teacher. When first, as insignia of office the Chancellor
was honoured with the custody of the Great Seal, as if
the very idea of condescension to a sphere of ordinary
and unostentatious Christian work were inadmissable,
a personal friend remarked to him that of course he
could not now continue to teach in the Sunday-school.
"*Why not?*" asked Lord Cairns —in a manner and tone
that were sufficiently expressive of decisive purpose.*

It has been told, when appointed Lieutenant-Governor, a report was put into circulation that Judge
Wilmot's Superintendency would be resigned ; and
that the oversight and drudgery of Sunday-school
would not be deemed compatible with the elevation
and dignity of official administration.   To some of the
young people, impressed with an excessive sense of the
grandeur to which he had been raised, imparting to
current rumour an air of probability, the matter was
one of serious moment.   A little fellow from one of
the smaller classes resolved himself, or was constituted
by acclamation of that somewhat extraordinary group,
a deputation to demand explanation.   After listening
with amused interest there was a positive assurance
that no such traitorous thought had been entertained.
He could never prove recreant to duty. The satisfying
intimation was also given that, " if by any possibility
duties were found to be incompatible and one of

* *Christian Herald*, London.

two offices must be surrendered, in preference to the
Governorship with its honours and emoluments, he
would cling to the Sunday-school."

In affinity with love for flowers and music was his
sympathy with and affection for sunny child-nature.
There was, beneath and beyond, belief in the boundless possibilities of their mental and moral being. The
children of the Sabbath-school were known to him by
name. In the most dignified company, without a
winning smile and a magnetic word of kindness, it was
not easy for him to pass them even in their dusty play
upon the street. It was a gratification of the very
highest kind to gather around him the early, beautiful
and unsophisticated sympathies of the little ones ; and
to control, touch " those chords so fine,"—

> " And tune their hearts too high
> For aught beneath the sky."

Did·not the feature of character, thus indicated,
more than scintillations of genius, splendid corrusca-
tions of speech, and brilliant successes of life, constitute his real greatness and claim to special tribute ?
Recently there was a review of the Austrian cavalry
before the emperor and empress. Just as a squadron
of hussars swept out from the main body of thirty
thousand horseman, a little girl not above four years
old darted from her mother's side in the front line of
spectators and ran on to the open field directly in front
of the advancing host. The squadron was at full
gallop. It was close at hand. The death of the child

seemed inevitable. A thrill of horror passed over the powerless spectators. The empress, a full observer of the scene from the carriage, uttered a cry of horror at the sight of the little one just to be trampled to death by a thousand hoofs. At the instant a trooper swung himself down from the saddle, along the side of his horse's neck, and catching the child lifted it with himself safely into his saddle without slackening his speed or breaking the alignment. The little one was saved. Ten thousand voices raised a shout of joy. The empress and the mother burst into tears of grateful relief. And the emperor, summoning to his presence the noble soldier, took from his own breast the richly enamelled cross of the Order of Maria Theresa, and hung it about the neck of the brave hussar.*

To the Austrian hero, for that intrepid act, the rescue of a child from a great and immediate peril, we gladly and cheerfully accord the very highest recognition. Boundless applause of spectators, imperial approbation and award, jewelled cross and decoration of an illustrious Order were all well and worthily bestowed. Through that noble deed a little girl had been snatched from the jaws of death. But are there no wreaths woven for those who, spurning selfish ease, are ever on the alert to save children with all their immortal destinies, from sin and vice and ignorance and other perils—more to be dreaded than the trampling hoof of Austrian cavalry? Shall not recognition of

* London *Standard*.

grandeur and of a greatness, due to highest and holiest heroism, be accorded to men and women who unselfishly minister to the least of the little ones? When famed and lauded distinctions of earth are forgotten, warriors' chaplets withered, gold of the millionaire cankered, storied urn and sculptured marble and glittering mausoleum wasted to dust and ruin, then shall service of Christ and self-denying toil for the welfare of souls obtain full and final recompense:

> "Thy feet shall stand on jasper floors;
> Thy heart shall seem a thousand hearts,
> Each heart with million raptures filled:
> Thou shalt sit with princes and with kings."

The department of the school to Judge Wilmot of special and unfailing interest was the Infant Class—which, as conducted in that charge, has been carried up to the very highest point of excellence. It was a class which of all others the Superintendent never failed to visit. The beaming countenances of bright children told of the genuine delight with which they listened to even his most commonplace remarks. To this class we may accompany him on the last Sabbath of his life: "Now children," he said on that occasion, your old superintendent will leave you some day and what shall I do if some of you fail to meet me up there? Why heaven will be no heaven without my children! I will just wait and watch at the gates of gold. If I miss any, I will say surely they have not strayed away. Some of our children have left us, and they are with

G

the angels now.   Then I like to think that they grow
through the eternal years.   Children will not always
remain children in heaven.   Their minds and forms
will develop there as well as here."   At this moment
there was a trace of disappointment in the teacher's
face,* for the shadow of a sore bereavement had fallen
upon her life, and there had been the cherished hope
of meeting the little one unchanged in form : " Ah !
well," he said, " you will be fully satisfied."

The consecration of service was not bounded by the
limits of one charge.   Representatives of the several
Sunday-schools in the City of St. John, "Church of
England, Presbyterian, Wesleyan, Baptist, Congregational," resolved to mark their sense of appreciation
by some special token.†   The reply of Judge Wilmot
was as follows :

" GENTLEMEN,—I receive with great pleasure the
Books and Diagrams which you have presented to me,
on behalf of the St. John Sunday-schools, for the use
of the School under my superintendence at Fredericton ; and for myself, and in the name of my beloved

---

* Mrs. Wm. Lemont.

† The following document, copied from *The Church Witness*, needs
no explanation :—

At a meeting of Superintendents of Sabbath-schools, in the City of
St. John and Parish of Portland, held in the rooms of the Young Men's
Christian Association, on the evening of May 25th, 1858.

On motion, it was unanimously *Resolved*, That we tender to his
Honour Judge Wilmot, on behalf of the Sabbath-schools, which we
respectively represent, our sincere and hearty thanks for the great interest he has manifested, at different times, in the welfare of our

teachers and scholars, and I thank you for your very valuable and useful present. •

"On the occasion to which you refer, I found an abundant reward *in* my work, and yet a greater reward *after* my work, in the assurance, that among teachers and scholars, a fresh interest was thereby awakened, not only in the *perusal*, but in the *study* of the Holy Scriptures. And as you have now furnished me with a bountiful supply of materials for future lectures, I shall look forward with great pleasure to the first favourable opportunity for again addressing the St. John Sabbath-schools; when we shall either traverse the 'Catacombs of Rome,' and explore the sepulchral records of primitive and persecuted Christianity, or make an excursion among the monumental inscriptions of 'Ancient Egypt,' and there read the hieroglyphic history of the captivity and deliverance of Israel, in perfect accordance with our own inspired history; or range the fields of 'Fulfilled Prophecy," and gather materials to strengthen our faith and confidence in the

Schools, and more particularly for the kind manner in which he met and addressed them during the past winter.

And further *Resolved*, That we request his acceptance of a Library for the use of the Sabbath-school at Fredericton, over which he presides; and also of four sets of Diagrams, as a small token of our gratitude and esteem.

Resolved, That Dr. Paterson and Mr. J. R. Ruel be a Committee to present these Resolutions, with the Library and Diagrams, to Judge Wilmot.

JAMES R. RUEL,   JAMES PATERSON,
Secretary.   *Chairman.*

Divine inspiration of the Bible ; or illustrate the de-
grading superstitions and barbarous cruelties of
'Paganism and Idolatry,' and contrast, therewith, the
benignant and peaceful influences of a pure and holy
Christianity.

"The statistics of your schools are highly gratifying
to me. What a responsible work! How incalculable
the value of faithful and affectionate instruction from
Sabbath to Sabbath to THREE THOUSAND TWO HUNDRED
youthful and immortal minds! Ever remember, that
loving, faithful teachers, are sure to find loving and
attentive scholars ; and the reward is certain, for 'in
due season we shall reap if we faint not.'

" 'The Book for both worlds' is THE Book for our
Sabbath-schools; and he who teaches the science of
Christianity from that *only* text book, may always be
assured that he never teaches alone, for He who has
promised that His Word shall not return unto Him
void, will assuredly accompany that blessed word with
the teaching of the Holy Spirit.

"Committed as I am for life, to the delightful work
of Sabbath-school teaching, I shall at all times feel a
deep interest in the success of *your* Sabbath-schools.
Our work is one—our *book* is one—our *God* is one—our
Redeemer is one—our *Comforter* one—our *throne of
grace* one ; and with all of every clime and kindred
and people and tongue who shall receive the final and
eternal reward in heaven, the *song* will be *one*—'To
Him that loved us and washed us from our sins in His
own blood, and hath made us kings and priests unto

God and His Father, to Him be glory and dominion for ever and ever.'

"Looking forward with much pleasure to the time when I may again be permitted to address your Sabbath-schools, and impart instruction with the aid of your valuable present, believe me, very sincerely and affectionately yours,

"L. A. WILMOT."

"Saint John, 25th May, 1858."

"Detained over a Sabbath by judicial duties, in the City of St. John, Judge Wilmot looked in upon us at the Benevolent Hall. There was at the time a feature of exceptional character, in the work of the School, which at once arrested his attention. The attendance of boys was in average excess of that of the girls. The promise was given that, if the same numerical proportion were carried through another year, a library of books should be presented for our use. At the end of the year a report was forwarded to Fredericton, showing that required conditions had been fully met. Accompanied by cheery and loving words, the books were duly received."*

Conscientious discharge of responsible duty found abundant compensation. Suffering from excruciating pain, a few months before his death, starting up from the sofa at the appointed time, he was at his post. "Years ago," he said, in answer to expostulation, "my work was attended to in that department from sheer sense of duty; but, now in satisfaction and accom-

* Superintendent.

panying blesssing, my comfort is rich and abiding." From the Sunday-school under his management, into the membership of the church, there passed a continuous stream ; and, from the same place, there were rich and constant accessions to the gathered ones before the throne. From young people widely scattered, often at the time of their reception to Church-communion, communications were received expressive of gratitude for the interest and affection of former years. These were results worth more to him than thousands of gold and silver.

" There were distinctions of another kind," says a Montreal writer, " and honorary appointments that he highly valued." * He was President of the Auxiliary Branch Bible Society, cherished a deep and intelligent interest in all its proceedings, and greatly rejoiced to be identified with a marvellous movement, the most magnificent of modern times, for the translation of the Word of God into the living languages of all people, and its circulation amongst the various nations of the earth.

At the Toronto General Conference of the Methodist Church of Canada, in September, 1874, Judge Wilmot was elected to the chair—subsequently occupied by the venerable Dr. Egerton Ryerson— of the preliminary meeting at which that important ecclesiastical assembly was organized. In association with the Rev. Dr. George Douglas, he was appointed to the Nashville General Conference of the Southern

* *Witness.*

Methodist Episcopal Church.* A rare deputation that could not have been readily duplicated! For who might presume to wield the Douglas brand or to bend veteran Ulyssus' brow? Had that united visit been made, as then was anticipated, the Dominion, as well as the Methodist Church of Canada, would have been nobly represented. One could have wished that for once, with unquenched fire of an impassioned eloquence, the Ex-Governor of New Brunswick had been privileged to stand in the presence of those Southern brethren.

At the Montreal meeting of the Dominion Evangelical Alliance, October, 1874, an influential assembly, in which Principal Dawson of McGill College, President McCosh of Princeton, Dr. Donald Fraser of London, and other eminent men took part, Hon. L. A. Wilmot officiated with great acceptance

---

* At the Montreal General Conference, 1878, in behalf of an influential Committee, by Rev. Dr. Anson Green, now also numbered with the sainted dead, a touching and beautiful tribute was paid to the memory of Judge Wilmot. The following resolution, formulated at the suggestion of Hon. S. L. Shannon, seconded by Hon. James Ferrier, was cordially adopted : "That while, for many years the late Hon. L. A. Wilmot, Ex-Governor of New Brunswick, occupied with conspicuous and distinguished advantage the highest position of public responsibility and influence for which, by the possession of varied and brilliant gifts, he was prominently qualified ; yet believing that the best efforts and most cherished sympathies of his life were, with unswerving loyalty, given to the Methodist Church, in recognition of his noble character, consistent life, and eminent usefulness, we gladly accord to his name and memory this expression and permanent record of our esteem and veneration."

as President of that body; and, "if deep interest
in the cause of the Alliance"—to use his own
words when taking the chair—"was any qualification,
he could claim a special fitness for that post." "He
thanked his brethren of the Conference for the honor
they had conferred upon him in electing him to the
position of President of this organization. He had
longed to be with them from the beginning of the
Conference, but was prevented by ecclesiastic duties
at home from coming sooner. He was happy to be
present and bear his testimohy to the necessity of
personal religion, of being like Christ in order that
they might all be one in Him, and thus contribute to
the honor and prosperity of the Protestant Churches.
He hoped that the result of this gathering would
be to promote the Redeemer's kingdom, and he was
sure that the world would be the better for it."

While loyal to the core, as a member of the Methodist Church, he was also profoundly and prayerfully
interested in regard to the prosperity and progress of
other denominations. He longed greatly for the existence and exhibition of a nobler spiritual unity.
Facts of fraternal intercourse amongst representatives
of the several Evangelical Churches in Missionary
lands, were perused with peculiar and grateful satisfaction. At a mass-meeting of the Evangelical
Alliance, lighting up the subject with illustrative incident, he made apposite reference to this subject:
"The Missionaries from the various societies laboured
side by side in the same field of toil. They were one

in Christ, and no matter of what denomination, combined together to meet the enemy. They had no time to discuss minor points of difference, for the enemy was pressing hard with a determined front; instead of wrangling over the Apostolic succession or other knotty points, they would kneel together, and, having invoked God's blessing, would advance shoulder to shoulder and attack the enemy. There was a fine illustration of such action in the British army. At the memorable battle of Inkerman, when the Russian soldiers, maddened with spirits, advanced through the heavy mist upon the British forces, and caused the right wing to swerve, several regiments were decimated in the struggle, and the survivors were obliged to fall back; and at the time Col. Kinloch gathered the *debris* of eight or ten regiments together. The men had been looking out for just such a leader; he rallied 150 men, in all uniforms; each man fell in alongside the other; there was no looking then for this or that company, or place, or companions, but every man stepped in to fill the ranks; and they had scarcely been told off, when a square of Russians charged, but the gallant 150 held 1,500 men in check; for they stood side by side and shoulder to shoulder, to do their duty, as faithful servants of the Queen should, to the last."*

"Before long," he wrote, April, 1876, in deprecation of some unlovely exhibition of exclusiveness, "we

* Montreal *Witness.*

G*

shall *in the church above* get past all conflicts of denominational peculiarities." He exulted in the thought
that, in heavenly song and service, they would ultimately meet and mingle in perfect and blessed unison.
That supreme ideal of Christian unity has since been
fully realized ; rapturous anticipation has been satisfied and consummated. Amidst the light and splendor of emerald and gold and burning sapphire, in fault-
less purity before the Throne of God and the Lamb,
the rapture of beatific vision and of unutterable communion, without a note of dissonance and with no
trace of the strife and din of earth's controversies, a
goodly fellowship, a glorious company, a noble army,
the sainted ones of all Evangelical Churches, and redeemed ones of every clime and name, unite in lofty
ascription ; and, in ceaseless and unwearied service,
chant their "hymns and holy psalms, singing ever-
lastingly."

"Grand, good, loving man that he was," writes the
Rev. Dr. Nelles of Victoria University, "how we
missed him at the Montreal Conference! We ought
to have some monument of one who rendered such
valuable service to the Church and to his country.
I recall, not only his noble career in Church and State,
but the pleasant hours spent at his home in Fredericton—when you were stationed there."*

The last Fredericton Conference was held in 1877.

---

* The Rev. President Nelles and Rev. Dr. Punshon, whose oratory
signalized the occasion, were at that time cordially-welcomed as
guests at Evelyn Grove.

The Revs. F. Smallwood, Jeremiah Jost, and myself, all from Charlottetown, were privileged to renew our intercourse with the family at the Grove. It was a most delightful time. One of the most delicious experiences of our North American climate is that of an Indian summer; then a deep and soft balm and dreamy haze spread over and suffused the face of Nature. Something analogous there was in those later months of the venerable Judge's life. There was an Indian summer of the soul, the genial warmth and soft glow of kind and devout feeling, richer, sunnier, and more beautiful than that of the seasons. How pleasant are all the memories of that last visit!

"Fragrant as the morn, as vesper fragrance sweet !"

The latest special effort of Judge Wilmot's active life was in connection with the new Cemetery of the Methodist Church.

"Besides many acts of beneficence," writes a friend from Fredericton,—for many years associated with him in the sacred intimacies and earnest activities of Christian fellowship and of Church work—"and generous contributions of which you are fully aware, he gave largely to various interests of the Church and Sunday-school. To him we are also mainly indebted for the Rural Cemetery—a beautiful burial-place of the dead. A few months previous to his death, for generous gifts, he received the cordial thanks of the officials constituting the Trust Board."*

* At an official meeting, June 11th, 1877, with special reference to

The thought has often returned : In what way can
the vacancy be efficiently filled ?   God buries His
workmen, but carries on His work; and the banner,
which fell from hands stiffened in death, has, we trust,
been caught up by others of like spirit and consecration.

The activities of the Judge's life were continued
to the last.   For a considerable period, previous to his
sudden departure, they were considerably chastened
and restrained by painful and threatening symptoms.
From *neuralgia,* in its severest form, he repeatedly and
intensely suffered ; but, the keenest distress, found al-
leviation and potent comfort.   When almost quivering
with nerve-pain, scalding tears forced from his eyes,
with a sweet smile, he would often say : " There shall
be no more pain; and God shall wipe away all tears
from their eyes."

"For the last few months of his life," writes a
friend, " his whole converse was of heaven.   Talk as
you would, on other subjects, he came back to the
same theme.   He loved to quote the passage : ' Eye
hath not seen, nor ear heard, neither have entered into

the Fredericton Rural Cemetery, in consideration of munificent contribution and of personal oversight, it was—

"Resolved, That the thanks of this Board are due, and are hereby
presented, to His Honour Judge Wilmot, for long and faithful service
in connection with this trust, for Christian zeal in all matters connected with the Methodist Church, and more especially for liberal
gifts and efforts towards procuring a desirable and beautiful resting-
place for the dead—which owes much of its present appearance to his
Honour's taste."

the heart of man, the things which God hath prepared for them that love Him.' The last conversation was upon the same subject : the glorious hope of heaven. The rapture with which he referred to the bright home beyond even then brought a dread and fear, of which we spoke when he had left, that the time of departure was at hand and that we must lose him soon. Through all that visit there was on his face a most heavenly expression. The last words on leaving were : ' *There is nothing true but heaven.*'"

My own correspondence with Judge Wilmot, with more or less frequency, was extended over a period of twenty years and was counted a valued and honoured privilege of life. The last communication, received a little while before his death, contains passages graphically and glowingly descriptive of the magnificence and brightness—the light and purity, the beatific vision, the splendour of jewelled masonry, jasper pavement, and crowns of amaranth and gold— of the everlasting city of God. It closes with the familiar lines :—

> "We speak of the realms of the blest.
> That country so bright and so fair;
> And oft are its glories confessed—
> But what must it be to be there."

That last line of the stanza quoted in many a conversation, like thread of gold or sound of lute, in light and sweetness, was woven into and mingled with an almost ethereal strain. "Yes," he would say, when admiration had been expressed for floral beauty, frag-

rance, or melody, in musing undertone or lighting
up with sudden flash of thought, " flowers are beautiful, music has raptures, earth has its joys. But *what
must it be to be there !* "

The " holy of the holiest leads." The gladness and
rapture of earthly service have been completed and
consummated in the richer, deeper, fuller joy of that
world where all saints adore, and all seraphs burn, and
all harpers harp, and all choirs chant. In one of the
last social services, in which I now remember Judge
Wilmot, he gave out the stanza :—

> " I see a world of spirits bright."

Heaven seemed nearer while we sang. The veil was
lifted to the vision of faith. With intensified fervour,
he caught the inspiration of that unrivalled strain :—

> " At once they strike the harmonious lyre,
>   And hymn the great Three-One ;
> He hears, He smiles, and all the choir
>   Fall down before the throne.'

To him, in thought and feeling, heaven was not far
away. To faith's aspiring eye its golden gates appeared. In converse and countenance there was that
efflorescence of rapt and holy anticipation which
affords the surest indication of a character and growth
of Christian life, ripening and maturing for eternity.
It is delightful, and yet almost startling, to think of
nearness to the spirit land. Between the Christian
and heaven *there is only a veil.* " A veil is the thin-
nest and frailest of all conceivable partitions ; it is

but a fine tissue, a delicate fabric of embroidery. It waves in the wind; the touch of a child may stir it, and accident may rend it; the silent action of time will moulder it away. The veil that conceals heaven is only our embodied existence; and, though fearfully and wonderfully made, it is only wrought out of our frail mortality. So slight is it that the puncture of a thorn, the touch of an insect's wing, the breath of an infected atmosphere, may make it shake and fall. In a bound, in a moment, in the twinkling of an eye, in the throb of a pulse, in the flash of a thought, we may start into disembodied spirits, glide unabashed into the company of great and mighty angels, pass into the light and amazement of eternity, know the great secret, gaze upon splendors which flesh and blood could not sustain, and which no words lawful for man to utter could describe!"* Suddenly, as we now remember, came the closing earthly scene. A slight concussion, a ruptured valve, a severed tie or tissue, a broken thread, and then the lifted veil, the ministry of angels, the home of the many mansions, the noontide splendour and consummated fullness and blessedness of beatific vision and of everlasting day.

The last Sabbath of his life on earth was spent in the usual routine of duty. That sacred day—its sanctuary services, hymns of praise, litanies of supplication, glad tidings of salvation, communion of saints, means of grace—always brought renewed gladness

* C. Stanford : *Foster.*

and hallowed anticipation. "One thing have I desired," he could say in fervent appropriation of inspired utterance, "that will I seek after, that I may dwell in the house of the Lord all the days of my life, to behold the beauty of the Lord and to inquire in His temple." Into the exercises of the Sunday-school he entered with all his wonted interest. The address at the close had some traces and touches of the old fire, for he was still eloquent. The subject was announced for the following Sabbath, and hope was expressed that there would be careful preparation. In his accustomed place in the choir, with unabated fervor, he led the congregational service of song. In evening worship was heard, for the last time, that voice of power and melody which in public praise had so often exulted up to the expanding gates of heaven. An arrangement was made for a musical rehearsal at the Grove for the following Tuesday evening. With all wonted enthusiasm, revealing the intensity of a life passion, he gave the assurance that "there would be a grand practice."

On the following Monday afternoon, in his accustomed health, driving in the carriage with Mrs. Wilmot, he complained of sudden and severe pain in the region of the heart, thought to have been occasioned by a seemingly slight accident, caused by an impetuous movement of one of the horses. He was at once driven home, and a physician summoned; but it was too late for medical aid. The golden bowl was broken; the silver cord was loosened. With scarcely an articulation he passed away. His departure was translation rather than death. The sun of his life set in a clear and serene sky, to rise in the sacred, noontide brightness of unclouded, everlasting day. *There shall be no night there !*

Thus ransomed ones—" the sacramental host of God's elect "—are " ever ascending with songs most jubilant from the faithful performance of earth's lower ministers to the perfect service of the upper sanctuary, with its perennial and unhindered praise. They are passing up through the gates of the morning into the city without a temple ; and it is for other fingers than ours to weave the amaranth around their brows." *

Rapidly the tidings of his death passed through the city. The stern fact, which for a moment it seemed impossible to realize, speedily threw the shadow of a deep bereavement over every home. Swift and sudden that departure seemed to others ; to himself the event had been one of calm and confident anticipation. There were tokens that he was nearing the home of the many mansions ; very rapturous were the visions of faith. He had nothing to do at the last but to step into the chariot and " sweep through the gates."

In a beautiful cemetery, in the suburbs of Fredericton, bounded on one side by the majestic river St. John—fringed and bordered by a rich, almost tropical culture—surrounded in adjacent park and slope with grand and graceful trees—a great concourse of people were gathered in the spring of 1878. From the stately

* *North British.*

church-tower—which, with heaven-piercing spire,
bathed in cloudless radiance, gleaming like a pillar of
light, crowns the loveliest of eastern cities—in slow
and solemn tone, the bell tolled out a funeral requiem.
They were met, those mourning ones, to commit to the
dust the mortal remains of him who for long years
had been closely identified with every prominent
movement of the community. Even that quiet resting-
place of the dead, in which he had planned and directed
to the last, and which now looks tranquil and exquisitely attractive, was a memorial of his taste and
enterprise :—

> " With silent step and thoughtful brow
>   All of the human left us now,
>   They carry to that peaceful grave."

But *mors janua vitæ* : " death is the gate of life."
That sepulchre is the pathway to immortality. Beyond
the gloom of the grave there is a life which never
dies ; and, in sure and certain hope of a glorious resur-
rection, earth is committed to earth, dust to dust, and
ashes to ashes. "When Judge Wilmot died, a brilliant
provincial luminary was suddenly extinguished. The
simple appreciation of the talents of such a man and
the good he did, apart from his political achievements,
should have led long since to some public action being
taken to perpetuate the memory of one of New
Brunswick's noblest and truest patriots."*

* Fredericton *Reporter*, October 13th, 1880.

For less of lustre in life and life purpose, and for public services less distinguished, there have been men honored with the magnificence and solemn pomp of national sepulchre. But all that was mortal of this illustrious and revered Colonist, as was most meet, was rendered to the mould hard by the city where his active and beneficent life had been spent.* And grudge not to others the trophied tomb or storied urn. To him on that day was paid a rare, touching, and beautiful tribute. A procession of some hundreds of young people, members of the Sunday-school, moved silently past the grave; each one dropped a flower, dewy with tears, upon the coffined dead. There was a deep pathos in that closing scene; hearts palpitated as with a sense of personal bereavement; there was a low murmuring in the air, "as the sob of an infant pierced with pain." That expression of tearful, heartfelt homage, more costly than glittering mausoleum or the gold of a millionaire, was such as few magnates of earth could have commanded; and the conspicuous merits, to which that unique and beautiful recognition was accorded, will, for a long time to come, constitute a treasured and influential memory.

* "This Province should have some memento of the men who in past years did so much for it, one of whom passed away a short time ago and who bore the distinguished name of Charles Fisher. Another was the late Hon. Mr. Wilmot, a man of the most brilliant parts. Some memento of these should be placed in the halls, not only as a tribute to their memory but to stir up national feeling and inspire others to follow their example."—*Speech of William Elder, Esq., M.P.P., in House of Assembly, February, 1881.*

It was a rare honor to, and a nobler memorial of
their comrade, La Tour d'Auvergne, the first grenadier
of France, as he was called, foremost in a land of
chivalrous deeds, when after his death his former companions insisted that his name should not be removed
from their record. Regularly, at the regimental roll-
call, it was answered by one of the survivors. There
was still an inspiration in the greatness of his life and
the thought of unsullied and heroic deeds. His name
of renown they would not willingly let die. Judge
Wilmot has finished his earthly course ; he was ever
foremost in the ranks ; he died at his post. But his
name cannot yet be erased from the roll of the sacramental host. His life, brightened and ennobled by
high and honourable service, will be perpetuated in
potent and enduring influence. *By it, he being dead
yet speaketh !*

In fitting memorial of an illustrious superintendent,
a portrait by a competent artist, to which members of
the Sunday-school contributed, hangs in the basement
of the Church. If not, like the warrior of Breton
birth, named at the regular roll-call, from that speaking canvas he looks down upon the assembled school.
He seems yet to mingle with the scene of earnest and
active Christian work :—

> "Nothing can bereave him
> Of the force he made his own.
> Being here and we believe him
> Something far advanced in state,
> And that he wears a truer crown
> Than any wreath that we can weave him."

Over that grave on monumental erection—prominent amongst memorials of sculptured granite, or of polished marble—in that burial place of the river plain, *In Memoriam,* a simple but suggestive and significant inscription has been chiselled. In contains only name and date and characteristic passage from the thirty-seventh Psalm:

THE HONOURABLE

LEMUEL A. WILMOT, D. C. L.

Born 31st January, 1809.
Died 20th May, 1878.

———

" The mouth of the righteous speaketh wisdom ;
The law of God is in his heart."

GUARDIAN BOOK AND JOB PRINTING HOUSE, 4 COURT STREET, TORONTO.

www.ingramcontent.com/pod-product-compliance
Lightning Source LLC
Chambersburg PA
CBHW031114020726
47495CB00007B/2194